Sex and the Single Cosmonaut

Also by Ishmael A Soledad

Short Stories

Hawking Radiation (2018)
ISBN 978 1 9763743 7 1

Novels

Sha'Kert (2021)
ISBN 978 1 8382594 0 2

Sex and the Single Cosmonaut

Ishmael A Soledad

SECOND EDITION (2023)

ISBN (Paperback)   :   978-0-6487125-0-3

DEDICATION

For Kitty.

To all the part time writers
making time between children,
family, work, or sleep.
It's worth it.

ACKNOWLEDGMENTS

Cover photographs courtesy NASA

TABLE OF CONTENTS

ROOF O' GREEN

I'M DRUNK. HELL, I'm worse'n drunk and beyond, even the damn white bitch Miley Cyrus muzac floating through the smoke sounds good. Cyril's laughin' at me across the pile of empties, I know he is even as he's layin' face down I can see his back shake, fingers twitchin' round the neck of his Bud, damn black fool, damn black fools the both of us. Fool maybe, friend for sure. When he's home she'll tear him a new one 'cause of me, out drinkin' an' bitchin' until he don't know which ends for shittin' and which ends for spittin'. Keeps me from Kath while he's like this, trod on, down, like my daddy but he didn't stay away from mom when he drank an' I aint goin' there with Kath, no man, I gets like this I go grab Cyril an' we hit it till I sleep out in the back forty at his place an' he gets poured home. She hates it but she'd hate the other worse, she don't know but she would.

It's time he went, time I went, I'm wavin' at the barkeep but why's he on the roof laughin' at me, he's lookin' at me but he's poppin' in an' outta focus, why the hell can't he stay still dammit?

"Ok TC, whadya want?"

His eyes are funny, sorta bloodied an' wobbly all three o' them, it's hard to know which ones lookin' at me. I grab Cyril's head – I think, I mean it's hair I got in my hand an' I can't pull it out tho' I'm tryin' – an' wiggle it at the barkeep "s' nows getta hom a wit him" an' let go of it, bouncin' like a pineapple all stubby and wiry like.

Cyril's still laughin' as I'm layin' in the pickup goin' cross town, fairy lights on the street lights dancin' in time with the exhaust an'

Cyril's manic drummin' on my guts ratta — tat — tat — ratta — tat swayin' left an' right, now starlight only warmin' me, colored rainbow dots no white so beautiful soft.

Cool quiet dark, my hands soft on grass sod no wind, no light the field back o' Cyril's I'm lyin' peaceful, this peace the only peace I knows the only one I knowed, between wors'n drunk and wors'n sober all my miserable shit life. Kath don't know it an' Cyril don't know it an' I don't tell no one 'cause everything I've ever said I hads been taken away and aint no one takin' this, no one not even that smartass genY doctor an' his liver prostrate death an' anyways it's worth it, just worth it for the hours a week.

I lose myself, I'm losing me, I'm glued to the roof o' green and sod and field and planet holdin' on so's I don't fall into the black and the beautiful lights, the stars, the empty but not empty but I wanna dive, dive out an' sink, sink forever like I belong 'cause it aint here's my home but she, an' she don't know she can't know cause I can only say it when I'm like this and I can't see her when I'm like this so she's not gonna know ever.

They know, they see, they call an' they come, their light spirals down, purple red gentle, silent unseen but to me an' the sod an' the field an' the roof o' green an' my fingers dug to the knuckles to hold me on, their hands on my head an' faces smooth, black as the sky and beautiful, "come home, come home now" they breathe, I cry my tears as fire I can't, I can't Kath, heavens hell without you an' hells home with you an' I can't.

My tears are theirs, their tears diamonds from onyx, cascading jewels rising to my chest on the sod on the field on the roof o' green, soaking as they whisper "it's alright, we'll wait, we'll be back and wait till you're ready" an' I know they will, they will, an' one day I will, I will …

… one day I will.

END

FINDING THEM

THE CAFÉ RESTED between early morning workers and the lunch time blitz of tired shoppers. It was my time, those few hours where a quiet table could be had to linger over a cup or two, watch the world float by without the waitresses shuffling me along for better paying customers. The barista was less rushed, more attentive, able to be cajoled with smile or kindly word into a better, richer brew, although the constant change in faces meant new connections, new people, new cajoling. These lazy pleasant mornings had become cultivated habit, and in particular I looked forward to Tuesdays. Tuesday was Keith mail day.

Keith and I had been friends for more years than I cared to remember, from sharing a flat at uni through children and relationships to our now approaching later years, only distance separating us. I had always thought of him as the brother I never had. A strange brother it is true, singular with many arcane and peculiar habits. Although no luddite he considered email the lowest form of communication, a convenient substitute for real thought and what he termed 'the beauty and prose of the English language'. It was not a position he had come to recently, but rather one bound to him when we first met.

"Josh," he once announced many years ago as I sat hunched over keyboard "just when will you realize how impersonal and dehumanizing email is?"

I tapped send then looked up.

"Huh? What are you on about?"

"Anyone can hammer out a note on a keyboard. If you really do value someone you'd make the effort to write, to spend the time with ink and paper like me."

"You?"

"Yes, like me," waving his fountain pen "like I do to people I really value. If you get email from me it means I don't really care, you're just one of the uneducated masses."

True to his word, year in year out he had written to me regularly, pen and paper, paper in post, and I had responded in kind. I had learned that even if he received an email he would respond in writing if he deigned the sender worthy. If the reply was in an email well, the recipient hardly figured in Keith's universe.

So every second Tuesday I would receive Keith's latest letter, a few sheets of tight but immaculate scrawl on his favorite bond, and sitting with my coffee read, reminisce and reply. One small ritual in a life built on small rituals, as are all lives. Keith had begun to wax lyrical in his latest letters, emptying the contents of his mind on paper, so this Tuesday the slightly bulged envelope was no surprise. Once he had disposed with the usual pleasantries of family, kith and kin he continued.

It has taken longer than I thought. It all started out as a bit of a mind game, something safely Quixotic only to have it translate to possible then probable then in some strange trick of osmosis or transmutation here it is, solid in front of me. I've been working sporadically on this particular problem for well-nigh 30 years now and it's only recently that the final pieces have fallen into place. They have played their game well but they don't understand how our minds work, or what true, soul consuming obsession is. That is of course not their fault, in fact they could even be working on it now and I wouldn't know.

The seeds were planted when I was very young, fueled by that old standby, television. Dad's pass time was 1950s/60s science fiction and at that age I didn't do too much reading, but the regular and sustained diet of cable TV did exactly what cable TV is designed to do, get me hooked. From a bedroom decorated with plastic rockets, Godzilla posters and Star Wars sheets through to calling my dog Adama I was hugely and irrevocably addicted, even to the point where when I should have been chasing skirt I was chasing the latest resin War of the Worlds model kits.

It was a science class and Drake's equation that set me off. Here was a way to work out the probability they were out there my teenage brain thought, and I willingly whiled away my time running through numbers and assumptions of ever increasing complexity, concluding that the exact odds were anyone's guess or, more correctly, anyone's assumption. Too much slack in the variables, too much room in the assumptions and too much space time in space time I thought. So, unable to assign a number to it all I decided to do the next best thing, find them. And there you have it, me knowing and accepting it was impossible but then blithely setting out to do it. Just like Winston's double-think without Victory Gin. Or room 101.

He moved on to other things leaving me hanging yet again in midair in his typical, irritating habit of going part way then halting, opening the door a crack but refusing to fling it open in one movement.

Which left me both intrigued and in suspense over the following fortnight, all of which was made the worse by yet another change in barista. Again the gentle nudges to be given about my table, my coffee, and the usual interminable questions about me and my life. Sadly, I wondered how any of them managed to finish barista school. I stood up and took my coffee back.

"Excuse me Miss, the coffee's not right. I ordered an espresso not a long black, and the coffee is too weak."

She regarded me curiously, as if criticism of any kind was out of her experience. It was gone in a flash, replaced by a courteous, if off the shelf, smile.

"I'm sorry, I'm just getting used to the machine. I'll make you a fresh one, won't be long."

She had a strange accent. I leant across, stared at her badge.

"Thank you Carmelitta. Where are you from?"

Her smile softened, head tilting to one side.

"It's actually Carmella," tapping the badge then moving to the coffee machine "they've spelt it wrong. I'm from Belgium, only been here a month. I'm studying and doing this to pay the bills."

I smiled back.

"Belgium. You must like your beers then?"

She kept facing away, watching the coffee filter through.

"Beers? Can't say I've ever met any of them."

It was a curious thing I mused as I settled back with my replacement coffee. A Belgian uninterested in beer, but if the coffee improved what did I care? And after a week or so Carmella and her coffees settled down and my routine re-established itself.

Again, another Tuesday, another letter from Keith.

So why would they be here? I settled on three possibilities, conquest, trade or curiosity. All three seem reasonable, the only question was which one? Conquest was simple, and on the assumption that if you could cross a few million light years you could easily wipe out a lesser civilization, I figured we would not stand a chance. A bit like the Incas vs the Spanish. And not sitting in a pile of radioactive dust I guessed it had not happened, so I dismissed it from my mind.

Trade was harder, having more potential than the first. There are myriad different ways to trade and it's possible to do it and not be seen. It was a real possibility and for a while I could not see past it if – and I had no reason to think otherwise – trade was a universal activity. Even if it was done in collusion with government, or hidden from public view, why not? Although possible I did think it unlikely as we probably did not have anything to trade. What could we have that they would need, and even as the question was asked I knew it was flawed. I couldn't know what they would need, after all value is a matter of perspective, so trade remained an open option.

Although this sounded plausible for a while, there was a problem – scale. They are not likely to flip across multiple light years for a single bag of rocks, or for even one cargo load. To make sense of the time and distance – not to mention the considerable capital cost, I mean think of it, it's not a Dodge Ram that's being hauled across space – you would need to think in hundreds or thousands of shipments. You couldn't keep that under wraps, worse yet if they just happened to want iron ore or coal or some other bulk commodity. So not having noticed a stream of large, silver metallic cigars loading up on bananas or petrol, trade went the way of conquest.

I was left with curiosity. Were they curious? How would I know? But it was the last option, the residual left to me. If I had a choice between a war, greed or curiosity driven stellar neighborhood I'd go curious each time.

The rest of the letter contained the usual family updates. I'd noticed that his writing was more compressed, less structured, not as neat as usual. Overwork or possibly excitement had perhaps got the better of him.

Tuesday week I came back to the café, Keith's latest letter in hand. A bit thin this time, holding it in one and pulling my chair out with the other, maybe he's busier than usual. I had hardly sat down when a smiling Carmella appeared with my espresso.

"Hello Josh, how are you this morning?"

It had taken me a month but she was working out fine, only a few rough edges left.

"I'm fine thank you. Nice day outside."

"Yes, warm and dry." She pointed to the letter. "From your friend again? A greeting card from holidays?"

I knew she wasn't being rude but was simply curious.

"No, not a card, a letter."

"Letter? What is that?"

For a young, smart, connected person – as this generation liked to market itself – she had some gaping holes in her general knowledge.

"Seriously?"

Even from her this seemed a bit much. Could she honestly not know what a letter was? How long had email been around, fifty, sixty odd years? Ok, maybe it's possible, maybe she's never seen a letter, never written one. I sighed.

"A letter, Carmella, is a message from one person to another, put on paper, then physically delivered to that person. Like a hard copy of an email."

"Sounds very slow, something maybe only old people do?"

Her manners were the next focus of my training. But not now, I needed my coffee.

"Perhaps. Maybe yes. I'm not totally sure. Thank you." bowing my head dismissively.

I took a quick sip and opened the envelope. This time there were barely two hurriedly scrawled pages jammed carelessly inside.

Josh

You know this all started as a mind game playing with assumptions and probabilities, but it hasn't finished that way.

It's taken until yesterday but I have the answer. I tried to imagine myself as them, curious and different. What would I do? With advanced technology I could sit and watch, monitor, learn, but it's like learning about home from what's on CBS or Facebook, a distorted picture. They'd have to be here, on the ground, in the thick of it. If they are totally unlike us, or can't make themselves look like us, then it's not possible. They might rely on spies, maybe advanced robots, whatever, but in that case they would not be here.

But what if they can? What if they appear human, or close enough not to be noticed? Would they come down for a look, to observe, to study us? Of course! After crossing those stupendous distances why stumble at the last hurdle? So given this, given their desire and knowing nearly nothing of the society they are observing and none of the nuance and subtlety of human interaction, how could they live amongst us anonymously?

They would need to appear normal, maybe middle class, maybe migrants to cover their awkwardness. Just staying at home or in one place would never do, they would be itinerant or at least highly mobile. They must work to get broader contact with more people, more variety, more types, different attitudes. Jobs where they get to listen or ask, jobs where no one asks them too much, pries, or they have to study. Not too menial so they can pursue their main goal; not too isolated so they have people around; not too deep or meaningful so they can't be discovered, the human shell they adopt being shown hollow. Something where coming and going is normal, rapid turnover, but is in the heart of society. Invisible perhaps, maybe part of the wallpaper, able to disappear unnoticed and traceless if suspected.

I know where they are. And who they are. And this afternoon my friend I will find out. I will find them.

The letter was postmarked Monday morning. I laughed, imagining Keith accosting some poor builders-laborer or cleaning lady with accusations of nefarious extra-terrestrial activity. Even on his high horse Keith was not threatening, merely amusing in a Daffy Duck-ish manner. Still chuckling an hour later I headed for the door, leaving my coins on the table. Carmella gave me a quizzical, questioning look then silently turned away.

Wednesday morning was my work morning. Laptop in hand I sat down at my usual table, the café unusually quiet. I was the only customer for which I was thankful.

"Buenos dias señor. ¿Que te gustaria?"

"Café. Espresso y agua por favour."

I looked up into a young, tanned face.

"You're new here?"

"Yes. I am Heraldo. Forgive my using Spanish, I am only one week in your country."

"You are from," and I hesitated "Mexico?"

"Oh no," laughing "from Madrid."

"Ah, the coffee should be excellent then." Perhaps, depending on how much training I had to give him. "Tell me, Carmella, is it her day off?"

"I do not know this person but I am only here now so perhaps later?" He started away from the table, pausing briefly. "Keith is no writing you today, yes?"

"No," I replied absent mindedly "it's not Tuesday." Something inside my head clicked but was cut off by a chime from my laptop. An email from Adele, Keith's partner.

Hi Josh

If Keith gets in contact let me know asap. I can't raise his mobile, he usually lets me know but he's been preoccupied lately.

He's been gone since Monday lunchtime, had an appointment I think at the Café Royale downtown.

Adele

I sat frozen. He must have finished the letter to me, gone out and posted it before going to the café … to find them.

I felt chill, coldness growing from the base of my spine. My laptop died, and in front of me the café's storm shutters started to close. I turned. Walking slowly, deliberately towards me, faces fixed and unsmiling, were the beings I knew as Heraldo and Carmella.

I closed my eyes, waiting.

I too had found them.

END

MARS HENCE

THE DESERT SLEEPS, afternoon shadows reaching from low dunes to embrace an infinite russet red landscape of sand and stone. Can't see anything moving out there, roos, birds, nothing from horizon to horizon. If it doesn't rain soon Dad will have to truck water in, more trouble and money poured down this wreck of a farm.

Mars just isn't the place it used to be but that's the gig and I'm living it. Paige casts a weary glance around the hab, across patched and rigged shelving back to the floor, back to the to the boots she's struggling to clip onto her suit. All well and good when I was thirty, an adventure for a lifetime but not like this. Should be more of us, more habs, more shots, that was the plan, the deal. She catches sight of a fraying pair of gloves placed carefully near the airlock, bright blue showing through rust red dirt. Hell Owen, why did it have to be you and not Gav?

It's getting darker, colder, I'll need a blanket or two soon to keep off the chill. The ceiling feels close, walls browned and pitted, my pillow's hard, my bed's hard. I can see Dad in the mirror, he looks worn out, tired. It doesn't matter I'm out of here soon, come my eighteenth. College then the dream, following Armstrong and Gagarin but further, higher.

The recycler won't fix itself, no use grumbling and anyway it's a chance to get out, walk on the surface again, live the dream. Ha! They don't tell you at induction living the dream means being elbow deep in someone else's shit. More time, less spares, you never know what you can do unless you must. Nearly suited up, only gloves and helmet left, she raises her arm in front staring at patchworked sleeves of bright blue and orange on silver-gray. At least I've managed to keep two suits going, not the prettiest but functional enough, enough to last. Raising her left wrist closer she squints through her glasses, straining to make out the dial. In the green, maybe two, two and a half hours O^2, should be enough.

I'm getting hungry and tired but all the same waiting for the night, the stars and the quiet stillness just to sit cocooned and warm against the cold. Where's Dad? I'd go out and look but Mum don't like me being out at night. I've only a precious few days left at home, what's she going to do when I leave?

All checked out, just drop the visor and go. Seems like the suit just gets heavier each time, I'm going to need a zimmer frame soon if this keeps up. She walks slowly to the hab divider, pokes her head around. It's not his fault, you know it's not, it's just the gene, just the luck of the draw. Another flip, another sequence and it could be you there or worse yet Owen then where would you be?

Mum's at the door smiling, she's old and bent but I remember her young, vibrant, happy. She's always sad now, it's hard on her and Dad, they've been through hell. She waves, I wave and she's gone.

Cycled the airlock and out, a tiny figure lost in the vast emptiness of Isidis Planitia. She's still shaking her head, keerist he's back in Australia again, well at least he's no trouble. The row of four mounds to her left pull at her, small cairns of rock topped by helmets orange, pink, white, bright blue. Maybe he's better off lost in his mind than here.

It's too cold, the kitchen's always warmer. It's barely big enough with just me sitting here, the table cleared and walls curving to an igloo roof, a small shack on the plain but home enough for us three. It's peaceful, quiet, not like our old place Mum never liked in The

Alice.

Taken me an hour and a half but it's done, again. Damn if I just had the spares but I don't, it's not anyone's fault they went bust but it had to be just after we arrived didn't it. Just turning up with what's on our backs, old time pioneers out west but with no iron horse back east. You'd think they could at least reply but silence, nearly thirty years of silence? She straightens, looks back at the four mounds. Two not strong enough to take it on and live, one too stupid to know we didn't want it to end as much as she did, and my Owen, too caring to let her go. The cone of light from her helmet dances in time with her sobs.

It's dark and they're still out, probably gone to the Kinley's for supper. He stands, heads to the door, uncertain. Maybe I should go see, I've been cooped up all day, fresh air and stars would be good. His hand goes to the release, hesitates. Mum'd be worried if she comes back and I'm not home. And she forgot to lock up, she'd be mad if she knew. He looks to one side, grabs a lever and pulls hard. He ignores the flashing red 'Lock Over-Ride Secured', it's meaning lost to eyes clouded and dimmed with age.

She plods back to the hab, a solitary silver-gray figure on endless dark plains, stars burning bright, pale blue pool of light guiding her way. Half of all humanity for 53 million kilometers, two septuagenarians one frail and barely functioning, one dysfunctional and dementia ridden. The child she never wanted, never had, never needed now thrust on her. She sighed. Not long Gav, Mum's coming.

Maybe midnight now and I'm dozing off. At least it's quietened down. What's with people banging on the door this time of night? Kept it up for nearly an hour before they went away.

Wonder when Mum's coming home? I'm hungry.

END

SEX AND THE SINGLE COSMONAUT

INZALI ARIBA

THE AIR CONDITIONER howls, it's only twenty-five celsius outside but it needs to be eighteen here, on the edge between comfort and freezing. Can't relax, be comfortable, let my mind wander. My pills knock me out for eight hours at a stretch but in the grayness hides danger. The numbers, I must crunch the numbers. Equations swim on the page before me, I must concentrate, derive and calculate to engage my logic centers, shut out the emotion, the noise. My models are ready when I tire of this, my word games next to them when I tire of the other.

Oh god her picture's still here why did I leave it? The crack opens, I know she's outside locked away from me, me from her. Numbers, concentrate damn it, concentrate! The crack widens and it floods me, I feel it all the suicides, violence, pain and heartache all too real. I slide off the chair onto carpet, the bottle spills from shaking hands as I swallow three, four, how many, jesus god when will it end?

Dappled warm sunlight fell on Inzali Ariba as she pushed another seedling into the thick mud, one of thousands before and thousands to come. The coolness of the paddy caressed her calves, the gentle wash back and forth a reminder of the other village women to either side intent on finishing to return to children, cooking, husbands. The rhythm of the day led her to daydreaming, imaging herself in school, out with friends, fine clothes and food, the normal yearnings of any fourteen-year-old girl. Inzali knew that for her these things would be out of reach, her village unwanted and unwelcome strangers in a country they had lived in for a thousand years. Maybe for her children or theirs it would be, but for her the day, the sun, the daydreams were enough.

The crunch of tires on dirt betrayed two trucks moving to the village, one stopping on the ridge above the field. A dozen soldiers jumped out, scrambling down into the paddy guns waving, shouting. Separated into two groups Inzali found herself with the younger girls, the older women and her mother herded together in tears. Three soldiers singled her out, dragging her up the slope into the jungle, laughing prodding each other, stopping a few yards in grabbing at her, clutching, propping her up against a tree.

The one nearest leered at her, face nearly touching.

"What's your name bitch?"

Shaking she opened her mouth, pointed and shook her head.

"You can't talk?"

She nodded, crying.

Another laughed, unbuckling his trousers to sounds of rifle fire.

"Just as well, we've got better things you can do with your mouth."

They threw her in the back of the truck with four others bruised, torn, sobbing.

"Don't know what you're crying for, think yourself lucky we're keeping you."

He slammed the tailgate shut and jumped up.

"Maybe you'd like to join the others?" laughing, the truck moving down the road past rose colored paddy fields and their strange plantings.

Feet on desk I pulled my mind back to the screens and feeds. I'd woken tired from broken sleep, tense and stressed and I just couldn't shake it. It wasn't me, I'd always strongly reflected other's feelings, but more some office colleagues who were out of sorts. I could see the pair of them looking frayed, haggard. Jeannie was closest, I stood up and walked over. I was barely two meters from her when she looked at me, scowled and wagged her finger. I shrugged, headed across to the other side to Brenda.

"Hey Brenda, ready for a coffee?" She and I went back ages, old friends we'd started here together. She gave me a look that would've frozen Hades.

"Only if I can drown your ass in it!" she growled through clenched teeth then, almost as if she only just heard the words, jerked back. "Hell Denis I'm sorry, I didn't mean to —"

"It's ok, I just thought you could use a break, you look like, ah, a bit edgy."

"Yeah yeah, guess I am." She frowned. "Just seem to be overly aggressive, nearly bit Ted's head off this morning."

"You're not the only one."

She jabbed the screen in front of her.

"Look at this."

The data was familiar, we'd been assigned the crims and cranks section of the paper and rotated regularly. For the past few months she'd taken the crime stats and police reports, I got the psychics, paranormals and whatever didn't fit elsewhere basket.

"Common and aggravated assault ticking upwards." Not earth shattering but interesting.

Brenda leant forward and split the table by gender.

"Now what do you see?"

It all looked normal up to a month ago but since then the stats went crazy. Male on male assaults had fallen, male on female dropping out of sight. On the other hand female initiated assaults had skyrocketed, but only female on male; female on female had utterly ceased.

"Interesting, what's behind it?"

Brenda was staring at the screen, her mouse in a death grip.

"Maybe you're just getting a taste of your own medicine." It wasn't said in anger, just dispassionate, cold, disturbing.

I stepped slowly back.

"Ah, maybe a rain check on that coffee yeah?"

"Whatever."

It was a nightmare that wouldn't end, why didn't Allah in his mercy end it, take the pain, the torture as she had begged? Three, then four, then one, shared as meat or a toy abused and raped again and again relentlessly, viscously, Inzali hated them, hated herself, cursed the life that had led her here. She hadn't seen any of her villagers since the truck, since being dragged from room to room, place to place. She shuddered from the cold water, tried to wash the stain and filth from her but could not. Alone for the first time in weeks she curled up, no tears left, praying for deliverance that she knew would not come, for a hiding place denied her even in fitful sleep.

She looked shattered, vacant eyed, mouth a harsh scar. One white knuckled hand gripped the steering wheel, the other a bare wire. The eyes refocused, hardened and stared straight ahead with disgust, loathing, menace. Tossing her head back she drove the bare wire into the roof. The screen flared white, black, then switched to another CCTV point. The van's sides puckered in as if to take breath then disappeared in a searing orange–white globe, hurling cars and people outwards, upwards. The glass walled office block over the car park distorted, quivered, then collapsed in a shower of dust, flame and crystal shards. Hot streamed from the paper's net tie-in I'd replayed it over and over watching TATA's regional headquarters and a thousand people instantly obliterated. It was three hours old, all over the networks, and here I was stuck with Delores herself, holder of the Nancy Reagan Chair for Paranormal Research at Cal State for what had been our regular interview.

I closed the laptop.

"What did you say?"

She looked over the top of her glasses.

"I asked if you could feel it, the oppression. How have you been feeling around your wife, colleagues, me?"

I shifted uneasily. I didn't like being interviewed, especially by someone who claimed to be telepathic.

"Honestly, a little twitchy, I must be tired or overworked."

"Tell me, the bombing, how many of those have you seen? I'll tell you. None, not by well-adjusted middle-class women. She's the first domestic African-American suicide bomber isn't she?"

"First I know of."

"She won't be the last. And the other things, the assaults, crime and the rest, it's unusual but you have no idea."

"Of what?" She was argumentative, a typical academic, but it made her fortnightly column that much more interesting.

"The pattern. It's only women, the increasing violence, rising anger, 'edginess' as you put it. But not all, not yet. You remember May's column?"

Couldn't forget it. 'Everyone's Telepathic' generated a tweet storm that still bubbled along.

"Well something's out there bouncing across the more attuned women, something unsettling. It's anti-male, it's growing, gaining strength, driving behaviors. The ones who aren't as attuned are just getting a taste. She," pointing to the closed laptop "was probably at the upper end like me but probably didn't know it. Even now it's a struggle not to get my gun out the bottom drawer and put a bullet between your eyes."

She smiled, mockingly.

"Not much of a struggle, but it's there. As for you, I've told you before you've got the ability, a strong ability, and it's getting to you. With us the anger points outwards, yours points inwards, sensitizes you to what's going on."

I didn't believe her before and I wasn't going to start now. I stood up, made my goodbyes and headed for the door. She pulled me up.

"Listen, I know you're skeptical but take some advice. Don't do anything to upset any woman, stay in the background and stay quiet for a bit. Try and detach your emotions too, it might help you settle. Hopefully it will all just blow over."

At least this time when they'd finished they'd thrown her in with others, with food. She found herself facing seven haunted faces, all clinging together huddled in one corner. One face was familiar, Malala, daughter of a village elder. They held tight for ages, shared suffering easing the burden if not the pain. Malala cradled Inzali's face in both hands, gently, close.

"My poor sister, what a thing has happened to us. No-one will come, no-one will save. It is true, we are all alone and have none to turn to. Listen to me, listen carefully," drawing her closer "to survive now is to win. You know they will come again and again for us?"

Inzali nodded.

"It is only our bodies they defile, not our minds, not our hearts. When they come, when they do, hide in here," squeezing her thumbs gently on Inzali's head "go into here and stay, make your safe place and stay, no-one can get you there."

Inzali nearly smiled, sorrowful, clutching Malala.

"If only you could speak my sister, if only you could." The key in the lock grated. "Remember, go here, hide in here, no-one can own you."

Colonel Li Cxi Cuin ground her cigarette out on the table, looked at her unit, the all-woman cream of the People's Liberation Army's airborne divisions.

Two dozen pairs of eyes stared back, not with the cold steel of professionals but the burning of fanatics. Each bore black rings screaming of lack of sleep, each one haunted and driven by a common waking nightmare. She stabbed the screen behind her.

"All right, it's now just the doing. Right here, the Myanmar / Bangladesh border, eight of them held by one unit."

In the darkness their transport waited, engines idling, cargo bay ramp open. It would be an act of war pure and simple, and she was leading it.

"Ingress here, HALO jump here, extraction at this point. We go in, take them out and bring them back."

Colonel Li stood, the room instantly at attention.

"Mount up, our sisters are waiting."

I just keep hitting him, straddling the bastard flat on the pavement, my hands screaming from smashing bone and flesh. I could feel him inside me, his mates laughing as they held me down, my turn now bastard payback bastard payback, your smashed teeth and broken bones not enough, not nearly enough. A brick to my right catches my eye. I grab it in my blood caked hand holding it ready, cocked above his head my wedding ring glistening … wedding ring? Pappa hasn't given me yet, the planting needs to be … planting? I shake my head, grimace, shake it again. What the hell, who am I? It all vanishes from my mind, I look down to the man I'm killing, a small barely conscious brown-skinned stranger. I drop the brick, stagger and fall shaking against a wall. Denis, Denis, what the hell is this? One minute I stopped to buy a carton of milk, next I've dragged him out of the shop, down the alley tearing the life out of him. Voices reach me from around the corner, I move away into deeper shadows, away from the man now on his knees. The voices turn the corner, transform into a small group of young girls laughing, joking.

They see him, one arm raised, begging for help. They run to him, stand around him. He looks up at a young blonde. She takes his hand gently in hers, smiles then gripping tightly sneers, yells, sending her heel grinding into his eye socket as he falls back. The ring closes, fists and feet in flurries, sickening wet snaps, shots then silence. I don't look back just run home, bolt the door and hide.

Inzali watched, detached, the men abusing her body. Malala had opened the door, she could hide, the pain and anger and hatred and humiliation soaked away, sent to Allah in his mercy while his daughter's body suffered. Her safe place in his arms, she would survive to yet be the pious daughter as her pain and terror flooded out and away.

Delores spat barely suppressed hatred down the line.

"I think it's a telaesthesiac episode here."

I'd locked myself away in my study, barring the door and windows. I could hear my wife pacing up and down, day and night, dragging my hunting knife along the hallway click clack click clunk across the door, the jamb, the shiplap walls. She loved me and I her, but I knew I was dead if I poked my nose out.

"Telae-ka what?"

"It's a transmitting telepath, we're getting what she's feeling. It's getting stronger, clearer, can't block it. It's not just the telepaths now, all women are getting it."

"How does it stop?"

"When you stop abusing us! Sorry, sorry, it's hard to control. We can't stop, can't block it. We see everything she sees, she's in a jungle

somewhere and the men, oh god they look like you! I can see them, I can feel what she feels its … its … sorry, look, I can't talk to you, I'm tracing the call I'm hunting you down, turn off your machine —
"

I tore the cabling from the wall, smashing my mobile until it was a pile of shattered plastic. Shaking uncontrollably I couldn't move, caught in the deluge of emotion from without and within, locked into the corner of the room in the dark. I clutched a paper weight in one hand, cowering, hoping like hell my wife didn't come in, didn't try, didn't make me …

Colonel Li smiled, flicked the safety off and waved two fingers forwards. They'd made it in unobserved, on time, on target. It was stronger now, she could feel them calling her. Twenty, maybe thirty minutes.

Inzali watched herself thrown again into the room, used and discarded. Her body was torn and damaged but she, her mind and spirit, was untouched. She rejoined, still and calm sitting next to Malala. Malala was twisted, bent, cigarette burns across her chest and abdomen coupled to cuts and bruises across her back. Her wrists and ankles bled, the ropes having cut hard, the smell of putrefaction wafting up. She looked up, lacking even the strength to raise her hands.

"My sister, we feel you, your pain as ours. I'm sorry, I don't think I have much left."

Inzali took Malala's head in her hands. She could not tell Malala how, but she could guide her. She squeezed gently, then left herself, looking down at the two of them. Malala tilted her head back, frightened as her body remained still. Inzali reached out, took her by the hand, then lifted her from herself.

"My sister, a safe place for all. Share yourself with me, I with you." and in that instant the pain and suffering of both women met, shared, and filtered away. Each was still their own, each alone but now shared openly, fully. "When they come again, as they must, we have our refuge …"

Delores woke up, sat bolt upright. Two transmitters? Yes, now two, and she could feel them. How? Telaesthesia contagion? How? Both together both in the jungle, both … she could see them, the first and the next, the names, Inzali, Malala, the suffering, the pain. She reached out.

"… and we will not abandon the others." Malala smiled. They looked down on the small group of women below them, reached out with their minds, Inzali the stronger leading, encouraging Malala until the six were with them as one, together, shared.

Malala felt it first, presences just on the edge, open and seeking, near and far.

"Inzali, can you feel them?"

"Clearly, yes, many. The more of us the more I can feel." Once one alone, now one part of eight, more than she could have imagined. She felt one strong close by, maybe two kilometers away with others, more across the mountains, over the oceans. In the far distance strong, calling, one above all others. All sisters, all being linked and drawn. "They have heard us faintly, some come to save, all are women … no, there are a few men, a few."

"We should try to reach them all."

"Yes, our sisters only, we must." and the eight reached out to the clear and the strong, then as they joined to the weaker and weaker until, in the briefest of instants every woman was linked, shared, knowing, feeling and seeing. In it all, unnoticed, one other was pulled in and shared. Unwillingly.

Colonel Li didn't break step or hesitate, one mind or millions, single or communal to her it was simply greater impetus to the task, her unit now truly one. Generations ago her forebear was Emperor Qin Er Shi's seer, the ability passing undiluted and unnoticed down the female line until awakened by Inzali. She reached out to Inzali, Malala, comforting, assuring deliverance soon, safety soon.

Delores reached out, caught herself, forced herself back to the place she was, the person she was. Too clearly she understood the latency released from Inzali when shared, compounded then transmitted around the world. She felt lighter, happy, balanced and for the first time in years the knot of pain and fear had left. Left for where? She forced her objectivity, tried to find it, somewhere in the linking, the sharing of memory and experience it must … and it was, outside them all but contained, soaked away and held to be kept away until or if it could be sent back. To who?

"To all those who have given it, to those who did not help us or helped them." Inzali clear, confident, powerful. "As I have given the burden to Allah in his mercy so my sisters, and as he has taken ours he has lifted yours. And it will be returned to those who sent it."

Delores felt around, saw the package contained, nothing touching it, alone but for one in its midst into which it was unfolding, copying itself, downloading everything into its psyche. Allah? Inzali's construct? She concentrated, recoiled, connected. Denis.

It's crushing me, tearing at me and I can't get rid of it, soaking in piece by piece by action by hurt all of it done by me to me for me on me with me. Act by act every pain and humiliation visited on woman by man, mockery to slavery and beyond, unfiltered raw loading on me and always in my name done to me screaming Denis, Denis, Denis …

"Denis! Denis! Denis hear me!"

"Delores? Delores, oh god I can hear him Delores how could I do it to you Delores —"

"Denis! Listen to me, listen!"

"Delores?"

"Denis, listen. Pay attention to me, to my voice, only me. Open your eyes, don't feel, don't pay attention to anything but me. Denis? Denis!"

"Yes, yes, listen to you, yes."

"Avoid emotion, concentrate on logic, numbers, reason. Stay awake Denis listen to me, do not sleep. Denis, what do you do?"

"Awake, listen, logic, numbers."

"Primes Denis, what are the first three prime numbers?"

"Ahhh, one, three, ah ah five, five."

"What are their factorials? I'm coming now, soon ..."

Colonel Li stood stock still one meter behind him. Bare chested, sweat soaked pants, cigarette in one hand Inzali's tormentor had no inkling of her presence. She fingered the blade, she could end him in any number of ways, slow or quick, the choice was hers. But not today. She saw the package and knew the time had come. The price of her career had been high; it was time to give them their own, to send it back. She felt her unit smile; Inzali, Malala and their village sisters agree; the linked world consciousness accept. She reached out, took the package and fully connected every man to it undiluted, unconstrained. For each one the entirety was theirs.

He fell to the ground, choking sobs caught in primal fear, pain, self-loathing horror, clutching his knees to his chest as were all Inzali's tormentors, and as here every man across the world. Colonel Li called for the airlift, stepping carefully over the impotent form at her feet. Yet a while would they suffer, until she decided they'd had enough. After release then justice, true justice and always the package hovering, threatening, Damocles' sword to control.

With no system to hide behind, no shield or cover and their lives on clear display to all, many cheated justice by their own hand. To the package pain upon pain was added, pain from the suicides, pain from knowing what a son, brother or lover truly were, from what was seen but not understood, what was understood but not acted upon. All this from they who would bear it to await sharing with those who inflicted it.

Except I. Drawn in by Inzali and Malala, fused by Colonel Li's connection I am caught, one with it never to be broken. They have tried, have drained and exhausted themselves for nothing. I cannot end it, to take my life will only add to the pains it holds and perhaps – if Delores is right – even collapse it back upon us all.

My life, such as it is, is to suffer. I stand as a totem, Cassandra, a life exiled in absolute solitude, disciple to logic and reason, sleeping dreamless sleep. When will it end?

END

SECOND MAN

"Might as well."

Ukko turned.

"If you like. What is it?"

Akka brushed one gloved hand over the engraved panel sending away a gray mist.

"Apollo 11 landing site, 1969."

He looked down from the perspex platform to the descent stage then up at the ascent stage.

"I don't like that."

"Why?"

"Well all this is real, their footprints, where they first stepped out. Doesn't feel right having a holo on top."

"Why's this important again?"

"First men on the moon, start of it all."

"Oh. Never was one for ancient history."

"Ancient history? Ancient history my ass!"

"C'mon Buzz, it's been a while."

"And you're keeping count Mike?"

"Not like there's much else to do."

He walked through the LEM's legs, tried and failed for the millionth time to smudge out Buzz's footprints.

"Four hundred thirty six years, fifteen days and eight hours. Ancient history."

Neil glanced at his Omega.

"Plus or minus ten minutes."

They left their own marks in the dust-coated perspex, smooth soled above rippled.

"Doesn't get much business."

"Not popular Ukko, no hero worship like back when. Everyone thought they were something else, role models, supermen."

"Seems to me the whole Moon thing's a dead end. The view is ok but Io, now there's a view. Or Titan. But this?"

"First steps, that's all. No real significance or meaning. Just flag waving. No one cares, I doubt if anyone ever really did."

Mike sneered, poking one finger through Akka's visor.

"Just get a load of long hair, I don't see your bio in Wikipedia."

"Well it's not like anyone did much afterwards. Six Apollos, a few others later then on to Mars. Can't compete with that."

"But this was first. Hell Buzz, being first matters."

"You're telling me."

Akka tapped the plaque.

"Typical late 1960's neurotic military alpha males. Take Aldrin. Hairy chested fighter jock on the outside, fragile as glass inside."

"So?"

"He was the second one out and couldn't handle it, spent his whole life trying to soothe his fractured ego. Always in the shadows, always justifying why, a compete social misfit who could only talk about orbital rendezvous techniques."

"Poor guy."

"You kidding me? Never good enough to lead a mission, never man enough to admit it."

"Hear this Mike? Fifty years no one's been here and now I get Mr. Never-Has-Been. A few missions over Korea and we'll see who's man enough."

"Don't let it get to you Buzz, it's the way things go, always paying out on what they don't know."

"I'd like to pop back for one second and straighten him out."

Neil wrapped one arm around Buzz's shoulders, led him back to the edge of the perspex.

"Everyone forgets, believes their own lies. If I had my way the ladder would've been twice as wide, we'd have gone down together. But you remember what those Grumman designers were like."

"I know, I know. At least I got here, better than Haise in '13."

Ukko stood gazing at the horizon.

"Was it worth it?"

Akka looked over Ukko's shoulder.

"All those billions to satisfy a dead politician's boast, bring back some rocks? I don't think so."

"How long after did we get the Drive?"

"A hundred years. Could've saved so much if they'd just waited. But that's ancient Americans for you."

"How's that?"

"Act now, think later, no patience. All ego, showmanship, each one believing they're the best regardless. A country of narcissistic prima donnas."

"Surely not all of them. What about their leader?"

"Armstrong? The worst. Aloof, snappy, autocratic, didn't talk to anyone about anything. Classic superiority complex. But that's not the worst."

"What is?"

"He used his position to be first. It should've been Aldrin."

A single ripple soled boot briefly popped into existence sending Akka skidding face first into the regolith.

"That's one small boot for man, one giant pratfall for mankind."

Neil turned, walked away.

"I'm going over to Descartes, see what Charlie's up to."

Mike set off after Neil. Buzz watched Akka shakily pick himself up, then hurried after them.

"Hey Mike, he screwed the pooch again."

"What?"

"Neil. He left out the 'a' again."

"I did not Buzz, you just heard wrong."

"You never got it right did you?"

"Well at least they remember what I said, who remembers 'Get your ass to Mars?' ..."

END

ONCE UPON A TIME IN THE EAST

OCTOBER IN VIETNAM is supposed to be relatively dry, but like everything else the country was trouble. Captain Dave Carvery disdainfully glanced from under the camo sheet at the drizzle. Three days straight, just keeping it sticky enough to be uncomfortable. At least he could cool his heels here, sit back and read the reports ready for November and the push into Biên Hoa. By then, if all went well, his company and the 173rd Airborne would have proven the value of long range reconnaissance patrols. He could imagine the looks on the faces of the smug bastards in the 101st when they finally discover he'd stolen their thunder. Christmas 1965 was going to be one to remember. He returned to his paperwork.

A small cough roused him, lifting his head to see a slightly built figure, poncho sending small rivulets to the floor. The figure removed its boonie hat and snapped off a salute revealing a 5th Special Forces badge on one shoulder below his brown bar.

"Lieutenant Tibbs reporting Sir." The voice matched the salute; clean, neat, fresh, by the book.

Carvery returned a casual salute from his chair, taking the proffered manila envelope and pointing across his desk.

"At ease Lieutenant, take a seat."

He scanned the contents of the envelope. One order, short and precise, that Lieutenant Tibbs should be given absolute cooperation for the duration of his visit. Straight from General Westmoreland's desk it was not open to debate. He placed the envelope in his top drawer and regarded Tibbs with a little more interest.

"So, how can I help 5th Special Forces? It's a long way from Nha

Trang."

"Yeah, and the airline food wasn't that good either. My team's here to uprate the Special Forces long range recon training syllabus. We have to make sure we've got the content right back at Recondo."

"You're here as observers?"

"No. We're here to go out on one of your platoon or squad level recons, then bring it back to Nha Trang."

"You'll excuse me Lieutenant but it's no place to send pogues. Maybe you'd be better off asking me what I think you need rather than just taking up body bags."

"We've all been active in country well before the 173rd left the states, we can handle ourselves. All I need is a place for my squad with your next long-range recon and when we're back we're gone, it's over. You're happy, I'm happy, Westmoreland's happy."

Carvery nodded slowly. What the hell, he didn't want more trouble and was too tired to really care. As long as my butt's covered if it all falls apart that's fine, and the General's orders were clear. He turned his hands over, palms up, fingers spread.

"As you say, we all want a happy General. Keith!"

His XO appeared shortly.

"Keith, Hobbs is taking Bates and Versteen's fireteams tomorrow?"

"Yes, 0415 for seven days."

"Tell Versteen they're not going, Lieutenant Tibbs' team will take their place. Find them some beans and dicks, a place for some rack time, then fill Hobbs in."

Turing to Tibbs he continued.

"The patrol leader, Hobbs, has equal rank. I'd expect you would find it appropriate to leave him in charge?"

"Absolutely. It's all about knowing what you need, not about me."

"Fine. Dismissed Lieutenant." and with a cursory salute Carvery returned to his papers.

Hobbs slowly clenched and unclenched his fists, stretching out the cramp from sitting motionless on the ground. Since 2100 the ten of them had sat, as they would until 0600, back to back, packs on, legs out in front. Six days in, six days of absolute silence, stealth and observation. Grudgingly he admitted the rabbits he'd found himself with knew their stuff and if anything could teach his guys a thing or two. He'd feared the usual cluster fuck when he lost Versteen's group but for once the higher highers got it right. Tibbs was ok as far as chucks went, and their rations beat his Cs hands down. No heat tabs, no dumb ass can of fruit, just taste you couldn't believe. They'd traded readily, Tibbs' group curious over the Cs and not at all keen to keep the cigs or gum. No matter what if even just these rations started coming his way from the fuss well, 'Nam would be that much more bearable.

Just turning 0200 he tugged gently on the string linking him to Tibbs. End of his watch, Tibbs acknowledging the change with a nod and thumbs up, Hobbs closed his eyes and lowered his chin onto his chest pack.

They'd slowly resumed the patrol through the two allotted map squares, closing in on the PZ. Strung out in a line they'd take a few steps, stop and listen, look around carefully, then repeat the dose in total silence. This 'still hunting' in the deep forest was surreal, even peaceful, with dappled light and mist rain from above filtering wetness on spongy leaf-littered undergrowth silencing their steps. Hobbs was on tail, making sure their tracks and traces were clean, Trúc on point dressed in VC gear carrying an AK47. Always good having him there, come upon any dinks they think it's one of their own, buys a few seconds in the confusion.

Hobbs' reverie was broken by Trúc signaling, a clenched fist above his head. By the time the patrol had dropped the bullets had started whizzing over Hobbs' head, pinning him 150 yards to the rear, scrabbling through the leaf litter. He caught sight of his men forming a skirmish line to the right and Tibbs' to the left, with maybe 20 VC ahead. Moving up he could see they weren't keen to engage, splitting right and left and trying to fall back. Trúc was heading deeper in, followed by Tibbs, the rest of the patrol fanning out. Hobbs was up and running for the right flank, catching the glimpse of muzzle flash off to the left. Tibbs might have been wounded he thought, watching him slow and fall back behind Trúc.

Even as he looked a squad of dinks appeared to Hobbs' right and by the time they'd been taken care of it was all over. A a quick head count came up one short. Walking to the small cluster around Tibbs he could see Trúc lying face down, pockmarked back rapidly staining his fatigues deep red. One of Tibbs' men approached and casually hoisted the body over his shoulders. Then in line astern, Hobbs now in the lead, the patrol resumed progress to the PZ.

The two helicopters skimmed fast and low just above the treetops taking the patrol back to base. Hobbs leant back and relaxed for the first time in a week, staring forwards through the plexiglass windshield at the slick carrying Tibbs and his fireteam. Trúc would be hard to replace but losing one of the rabbits might have been worse.

One of his squad leaned in, hollering over the wind and thrashing rotor.

"Boss, Trúc was taken out by one of the chucks."

"What's that?"

"One of the chucks, the brown bar, I think the fucker took out Trúc!"

Hobbs shook his head and turned to face him.

"Say again? You sure?"

"Sure I'm sure, the fuck I'm blind? I tell you I saw the brown bar behind him firin', I turn to take on the fuckin' dinks and when I turn back I see Trúc fallin' and chuck goin' over givin' him a fuckin' kick to make sure."

"You saw him do it?"

"No, hell no, I'd my own mother fuckers to do but I know what I saw."

Hobbs paused. Friendly fire wasn't uncommon, but was this fragging, deliberate? He remembered the last time he'd tried to take one of these head on. He shook his head.

"Keep it shut, I'll take it to the CO. We don't want none of that shit, we'll let him deal with it."

Carvery looked across his desk to Tibbs. The relative cool of early evening sifted through the hooch, a gentle breeze and ruffle of leaves, small clouds of insects testing their mettle against floodlights and DEET. He'd talked to Hobbs, looked at Trúc before Mortuary Affairs had taken him away and was still none the wiser. Friendly fire or frag, accidental or deliberate, only one man knew for sure and he hadn't said.

"Only one casualty, a good man. You saw it?"

"Yes, I saw him go down, I was about five yards behind him."

"How'd he buy it?"

"Not totally sure, you know what it's like, it was all over in a minute."

Carvery leant back, unobtrusively dropping one hand below the desk onto his leg.

"You know there's talk it's friendly fire?"

"Can't say that I do."

"It's not said casually, not the usual bullshit my grunts go on with. Another thing."

Tibbs angled his head slightly.

"Hobbs tells me your squad was good, very good. Maybe too good. I'd think having your asses glued down back at Recondo would take the edge off, but not so it seems."

Tibbs put his hands in his pockets.

"So we keep our edge, you know how it goes."

Carvery pulled the envelope from his top drawer, turning it end on end, tapping it on the desk in front of him.

"What do you think I would find if I gave Westmoreland's XO a call about this, or asked Mortuary Affairs to have a real close look at Trúc?"

Tibbs stiffened slightly.

"Some things are best left alone Captain."

"Perhaps Lieutenant but I'd need a reason. I've either got no trouble or shit loads of trouble and I'd need to know why I'm taking one or the other."

"So —"

"So level with me. You tell me what went on now, or you tell the Adjutant General in Nha Trang from a cell. Your choice."

Tibbs sighed resignedly.

"Ok, fine, but you'll hear me out?"

"Of course."

Tibbs bunched then withdrew his fist from his pocket, placing his hands across his knees.

"It wasn't the VC. It wasn't friendly fire. I took Trúc out deliberately. No accident, no mistake. It's what I was sent to do."

"Sent to do? Since when does the U.S. Army use hit squads?"

"Who said the U.S. Army?"

Carvery moved his hand down his leg to his holster, unclipping the strap.

"I see."

"And it's not what you think."

"Which is?"

"You're thinking who do I work for. It's the wrong question."

"And the right question is?"

"Trouble."

"Hmmmfff." The hooch was still, an enveloping thick silence warming stale, oppressive air. "I'm waiting Lieutenant."

"The right question is when, not who."

"When? I know when, two days ago."

"No, when do I work for."

Carvery screwed his face up. What sort of fool question was that? He coaxed his pistol quietly out of it's holster and slipped the safety off.

"When do you work for?"

"Correct. You wanted it on the level, so here it is. The when is three hundred years from now. I work for the future, your future."

Carvery's soft chuckle transformed into a cynical grunt as he bought the pistol up and trained it on Tibbs.

"Lieutenant, I've heard some bullshit before but this beats all. Why you killed Trúc doesn't really matter but you don't get out of it by playing nuts."

"Oh but Captain, the why is critical. If I say I'm from three hundred years in the future you can believe me." He looked around slowly through the open walls of the hooch to the camp outside. "Don't you think it's a bit quiet?"

Carvery smiled, raising the pistol until it pointed straight at Tibbs's face.

"Don't even think about it. This conversation is over, for now at least. Keith!"

"Keith!!"

Tibbs sat still, a sad smile forming.

Carvery's eyes betrayed the slightest concern, absolute silence being the only thing answering his calls.

"XO! Get your fucking ass in here now!"

"'No one is going to come Captain."

Tibbs' hand shot out and before Carvery could react the pistol was gone, magazine and chambered round lying on the desk, pistol in Tibbs' hand. Tibbs leant back, legs crossed, arms folded, eyes steady.

"Perhaps you will listen now. Take a good look outside Captain, tell me what you see."

Carvery cautiously shifted his gaze over Tibbs' left shoulder, beyond the hooch to the camp. The trees were still, silhouetted against the early evening sky. No breeze, no movement. Moths slowly circled the camp lighting ... Carvery's' mind took several seconds to realize that the moths were suspended in midair, small tufts of down dangled on invisible wires. He looked over Tibbs' other shoulder to a group of men around a small fire. Flames, men and smoke formed an image of still life, frozen rigid. Twisting, directly behind him his XO was locked in mid-stride, back foot on the ground, front foot suspended in midair. His cigarette balanced at an impossible angle from the corner of his mouth, glowing amber but stubbornly refusing to be consumed. He stayed transfixed for a few seconds then, subdued and confused, turned.

"How ... I mean why are they —"

"Honestly, I couldn't explain it if I wanted to, it's not my area. They tell me it's a bubble in time, we're simply going faster than they are."

He patted his trouser pocket.

"One press and the field is up, or I can drop you out of it and you won't even see me leave." He smiled. "Is this enough proof to get you to listen?"

"Ok, you're an alien from three hund —"

"No alien, I'm as human as you are. In fact I'm from Boston, or more correctly from what Boston has become. You ready to listen now?"

"Sure, go ahead."

"Right. My team's all from your future and we're all military, all Army if you like. Not strictly U.S. Army, but still what you'd call the 'good guys', Special Forces. We get sent out to do one thing and that is to kill specific individuals and do it in ways that are as invisible and unidentifiable as possible. People falling off cliffs, heart attacks, traffic accidents —"

"Casualties of war —"

"Exactly. Just as long as it looks normal for the time and arouses as little interest as possible. We get in and out fast, doing nothing to screw up the timeline."

"So who are you targeting? Dictators, despots, what? Trúc was just another dumb ass on the ground, what's he?"

"What was Trúc? He was one of us, someone who didn't like it then. You see we don't go back for people in their own time who do things we don't like. Think about it. Each time we have a change in government or policy a different set of people would be up for the chop. Give it long enough and no-one would be left."

Tibbs looked at the ceiling.

"When we found out how to time travel the temptation was to go back and make it right, or go forwards and see how we'd do. It took us a little while to figure out that would never work so we outlawed any interference, visits or even just observation. Eventually we managed to control the technology and put up a … well, I guess you'd call it a barrier, a barrier to the past and future that can't be crossed by just anyone. But it took time."

Tibbs pulled his gaze down.

"Trouble was that in that gap there were people, we don't know how many exactly, people who thought they didn't like it when they were and headed back or forwards to when they thought life would be better."

"And Trúc was one of them?"

"Yes."

"And he had to be killed?"

"Look, time and history are harsh, try to push them off course and they'll move but eventually they get back on track. It's just the how and when that's changed. So Trúc and everyone like him pollute history, they shouldn't be anywhen else but when they belong. Even just being somewhen else has consequences. And before you ask no, we can't simply take them back as that would change our future, a future in which they aren't there."

"So he dies just because he's here. Or is there more?"

Tibbs sighed, looked pensively at Carvery. Guess it can't hurt.

"Trúc's not the issue. He just wanted to live in a time with more rules and different morals. If it was just him and he made no difference there'd be simpler, less complex ways to take him out. It's his son. Decades from now his son denies someone membership of a political party. If she was admitted she would live the rest of her life as a harmless marginalized crackpot. Instead she forms her own party and leads her nation and this part of the world down a very dark path. So, we're sent back to take him out, to do it before 10 November 1965, before his son is conceived on R&R. The only way that worked was here and now, to make him a casualty of war."

Carvery and Tibbs sat in silence. Carvery looked again to the frozen world of the camp, to his XO leaning forward ever more improbably.

"Well ok, what do I say? It sounds nuts, it is nuts, but this I can't explain. But you've got one problem. You've told the whole bit to me so I know. So much for discretion and lose ends."

Tibbs smiled sadly, slowly reloading Carvery's pistol.

"Not quite as I see it. In less than a second of 'normal' time my squad and I are gone, we won't be found or remembered and all you will have is a story, a dead body and forged orders. You get two choices. One you tell the truth, all of it, and if things work for the best you get locked in a rubber room for a while until you are 'better' or they pin Trúc's frag on you and it's all over. The other choice you say nothing, tell no one and it all goes down as just another 'Nam statistic."

Tibbs placed one hand inside his trouser pocket, the other slid the loaded pistol back across the table.

"Your choice. Thanks for the beans and dicks Captain." with which Tibbs popped out of existence.

The noises of the camp returned, together with cooling breeze and smells. Keith appeared by his side nearly instantly.

"Sir??"

What do I say? Tibbs and his men are gone, Trúc's still dead and all I have is a story no one will buy.

"XO, make sure Trúc's effects are taken care of before we break camp tomorrow. Dismissed."

WU1 XV   GOVT PD   =   FAX WASHINGTON DC
DEC 04   630   PEDT   =   MRS ANNIE CARVERY

ROUTE 5 RAVENNA OHIO =

THE SECRETARY OF THE ARMY HAS ASKED ME TO EXPRESS HIS DEEP REGRET THAT YOUR HUSBAND CAPTAIN DAVID ARTHUR CARVERY DIED IN VIETNAM ON 8 NOVEMBER 1965. HE WAS ON RECON PATROL WHEN ENGAGED HOSTILE FORCES IN FIREFIGHT. PLEASE ACCEPT MY DEEPEST SYMPATHY. THIS CONFIRMS PERSONAL NOTIFICATION MADE BY A REPRESENTATIVE OF THE SECRETARY OF THE ARMY =

JOSEPH C LAMBERT MAJOR GENERAL USA   F48   THE ADJUTANT GENERAL   DEC 02 1965

DEC   05   920A …

END

THE OLD MAN, THE CAT AND THE TESSERACT

DANIEL MCWHIRTER WAS strange. He wasn't like other guys. He didn't go out, play pool, shoot hoops, watch Netflix, like porn or drink beer. Daniel McWhirter liked to read, real books, paper and ink books, books he could write in and on, dog-ear, spill coffee, read in the toilet, place face down open on the floor and load onto bookshelves until they groaned.

June McLune was normal. She was like her friends. She loved to go out, party, watch FoxTel, have boyfriends, sing karaoke and drink Tequila. June McLune loved movies, romances, big screen epics of tanned toned troubled and talented young men saved from oblivion and themselves by brainy buxom bucolic babes, loved word puzzles and alliteration and bad puns and laughing and sunshine and outside.

Daniel McWhirter was weird. He didn't like people, he didn't hate them but they were noisy and gave him headaches and heartaches and doubts and fears and feelings he couldn't explain. Daniel McWhirter liked cats, cats that sat quietly by themselves once fed, didn't need walking or explaining or excuses or promises or timetables or entertainment or talk. Daniel McWhirter had a cat, he called his cat Euclid, his cat didn't call Daniel anything.

June McLune was popular. She loved people, she loved the energy and noise and smell, the way she felt and they felt when she felt, the rutted musty smell of boy sweat and high-pitched laughter of girls. June McLune loved dogs, puppies, sloppy mouthed wet tongued shit machines that jumped or humped your leg and needed you, sad eyes and drooping mouth until the squeaky toy or stick sailed out.

Daniel McWhirter loved to think, think of shapes and objects and planes and dimensions that existed and couldn't exist all at once, of things of one dimension in six dimensions and animals that lived and didn't live in and out of time. Daniel McWhirter thought so much so hard so well sometimes the things he thought popped into existence.

June McLune didn't like to think too much, to hurt her head or dwell on things, she liked to talk and sing and stay happy, to keep positive and trim and good and awesome in a world of up and cool and friends and music and happy. June McLune wanted people to like her and be like her to feel the love and happy and awesome and noise and cool.

Daniel McWhirter lived in the apartment on the third floor where noise from the street faded away and the books on the walls shut off his neighbors and the kids across the hall were Muslim and didn't have TV. Daniel McWhirter didn't like the girl with the noise and the laughing and the friends and the parties upstairs, didn't like how she took away the shapes and the objects and the planes from his mind.

June McLune lived in the apartment on the fourth floor where the wind blew in the sounds of the jets through her window and the wafer-thin walls let in the sounds of families and love and happiness and the kids played soccer in the hallway at night until their parents dragged them inside for dinner. June McLune felt sorry for the man downstairs alone and quiet and silent broody not bubbly or social or living the awesome just living with a cat.

Daniel McWhirter was old and gray and wrinkled and crotchety and annoyed with the girl who knocked on the door with the fruit and the dog and the laughing and jabbering gibberish. Daniel McWhirter hated the way she now always lived in the shapes in the space in his head from the books and the planes for the things that existed but didn't exist.

June McLune was young and slim and eager and smooth and loved everyone and pitied the old man who hid behind his door and peered out his spyhole, didn't like fruit or dogs or Jay-zee or music. June McLune was stubborn and persistent and was going to make the old man happy and awesome and bubbly even if he didn't want it.

Daniel McWhirter wasn't evil or deranged or perverted just scared or shy and introverted and happy by himself with his shapes and mind and peace. Daniel McWhirter wasn't stupid or careful and between the shapes and planes and objects that weren't and are and shouldn't and spheres on Möbius strips in geometric precision on non-Euclidian surfaces in his mind the tesseract and the girl merged and swirled and danced and popped away.

June McLune was smart and brave and assertive and went through the door to the old man's apartment as it popped open and walked forwards and backwards and into and out of here and there and anywhere at all. June McLune was nowhere and everywhere and everywhen all at once with the sounds and smells and feelings of people and children all over and through and with her.

Daniel McWhirter was strange and happy. He wasn't like other guys. He stayed at home with his books and cat and shelves and silence and thoughts of objects and complex geometry cutting across and through his mind and space and time escaping out to the streets to the people and city below. Daniel McWhirter liked to read and watch the girl in the tesseract through the city in the people that smiled and danced and sang and partied and forgot to hate and lie and fight and thought it was awesome and cool.

June McLune was normal and happy. She didn't go out as no out existed it was all in and through and because of her and the singing and love as she danced in her place on the strip in geometric precision in the non-Euclidian space on the surfaces that ran through the tesseract that lived through the world. June McLune wasn't stupid or shallow and knew why and how and if but it didn't matter anymore.

END

A LITTLE KNOWLEDGE

ERROL HASKING HELD the clear plastic sleeve to the light. A near flawless nineteenth century one-pound note nestled inside its plastic sarcophagus, a token of one more chip in the walls of the black economy from a thankful counterpart. He allowed himself a smile. Even with the direst predictions cash remained, used and abused, without which he would be out of a job, out of a career and out of his calling.

"Looking good boss." Turning he could see Tanjya's hologram sitting, smiling at him. Only mildly annoyed he lobbed a crumpled tissue the two meters to the real Tanjya. Her hologram winced, then with a smile flickered out.

The real Tanjya dropped herself into the seat next to him.

"When are you lot going to stop playing with that?"

She leant across and added her virtual screen to Errol's.

"When the next toy comes around of course. Anyway, I've got something, part of the random check of BankNorth's cash transfers to the Reserve Bank, one of the tranches for destruction. Three notes were picked up, two tens and a twenty," the three appearing on screen "all from the one sub-branch in Darwin. They didn't show any apparent deviation except they were pristine."

"Pristine?"

"Utterly. All the other notes were creased, varying degrees of visible use and dirt, the usual cross section of wear and tear. These three however are absolutely perfect."

Errol reached into the screen and pulled out the nearest note enlarging it, rotating it, viewing it from all angles. In an act of utter futility he held the image up to the light before placing it back in the screen.

"Perfect."

Tanjya dropped the ten-dollar bills from the screen and pulled the twenty out. From the second screen she produced another twenty, pulling it out to hover next to the first.

"It gets better. Watch this. BankNorth's bill on the left, brand new mint on the right. Fabio," addressing the AI "bottom left corner focus ten times please."

The expanded bills now hovered above Errol's desk, stretching to the ceiling. In front of him the bottom left corners stood in relief, blue-green plastic crisscrossed with clear channels bordered in emerald green and light gold.

"Have a close look at the clear optic window section. Fabio, fifty times focus center edge please."

The scene shifted, two bright green lines bordering clear plastic now the only visible part of the notes. The other three team members now holo'd in behind Tanjya and Errol.

Errol leant forwards, examining the notes carefully.

"Exact match I'd say."

"Exactly, at the limit of our normal scans. How many perfect optic window reproductions do you recall?"

"None."

"Right. So that's why I got Fabio involved. You're not going to like this. Fabio, center optic window demarcation, five hundred times focus."

She waited five seconds.

"Fabio, five thousand times focus."

She waited another five seconds, eyes fixed on Errol. Small beads of sweat were now forming on his moustache, a twitch developing below one eye.

"Fabio, zoom extents fifty thousand."

She waited for a few moments, the office silent, the first drops of Errol's sweat falling languidly. She turned to face the notes, now bloated rectangles balanced on the desk.

"Resolution is now one one-hundredth of a micrometer centered on the lower left optical window of the twenty-dollar bills. I'd remind you that the image on the left is the suspect note, the image on the right uncirculated official issue."

Errol leant back in thought. In front of him one rectangle had a broad fuzzy white streak emblazoned down one side next to a ghostly gray field. The image on the left contained a crisp, razor sharp demarcation between perfectly opaque white half and perfectly transparent half. He shook his head.

"That's impossible."

"I know."

"Totally impossible, there's no way, physically no way."

"I know, yet it is, and yes I've checked. There's no way known to get crisp ink or polymer demarcation below one hundredth of a micron. We're talking clear separation at sizes approaching ultra-violet radiation wavelengths. But it gets worse."

"How? How can it be worse than perfect imitation?"

"Remember how this was picked up? Pristine bills in a pile of worn and tattered? I had one of the ten dollars sent across for materials testing, the results came back this morning."

Tanjya moved her hands through the screen, dismissing notes and bringing up a neatly ordered spreadsheet.

"This is the analysis. When you dig through the detail the summary is that the counterfeit note is does not crease, tear, hold dirt, is as tough as magnesium-tungsten alloy, and melts at just under 3,000 degrees Celsius. In short —"

"In short we could be screwed."

Errol looked around to his team.

"This stays buttoned up, no discussion outside ourselves. Tanjya, we're going to BankNorth Darwin. The rest of you I want in the Reserve looking through all the currency disposals. Tell them it's the ANAO, tell them I'm breaking your asses, whatever. I just want you to watch disposals, estimate the counterfeits and tie off any problems."

Errol's secure email tone sounded. It scrolled through on his right, Errol swearing vehemently under his breath. He stood and grabbed his jacket, stopping by Tanjya on the way out.

"Sorry to do this, you'll have to get out to Darwin by yourself. I'll join you later, just keep in touch."

"Yeah, no worries."

"Don't do anything more than look and learn until I get there. And no more cheap hotels, I want a place with working a/c this time."

Tanjya held her hands up in mock surrender.

"Fine, fine, a girl screws up once and wears it forever. I won't do anything, I promise."

Errol walked in to the Director's office, Karen greeting him with a brusque wave of her hand. He sat, answering her questioning gaze with one of his own.

"Less than fifteen minutes ago, same scenario, same features. I've got Tanjya in the field to track source, the rest of my team trying to gauge scale, and no answers yet. How many others?"

"At least ten, probably double that given lags. The Chinese, Indians, Europeans and Japanese have been hit. Of the second-tier currencies America, California and, if we believe back channels, the United Republic of Korea. And now us. It's not public yet but unfortunately the politicians know. You've seen it?"

"No, just Tanjya's analysis and pix."

"It's as good as I'm led to believe?"

"Better. Tanjya's had the ruler over them and they're impossible to detect casually. If we find where they're coming from maybe we can stop more coming in but with a dozen others can what we do actually matter? Have any others got any estimate of scale yet?"

"No to both."

"How much time do we have?"

"With the politicians in play three, maybe four days before it goes public. It could be sooner, the media has been trying our firewall a little harder than usual today so I'm thinking they have a sniff. We can't go storming around in jackboots until we know we can get a result, so it's just you and your team."

"As usual. Four days isn't much."

"For you it's less. You've got a meeting with the Prime Minister's Department in Sydney this afternoon so you're one day behind. Keep it discreet but once you have anything, a name, location, whatever, you call and then we'll go in hard."

"And just say we don't have anything by then?"

"Pray and hide. I will."

Errol wasn't fond of Sydney, his sleep at best fitful and fleeting. He wasn't a hotel person, he liked his own bed, his own partner, his own sheets.

Around 3:00 am the chiming of his proximity alarm woke him. Sitting up he could make out a pink rabbit at the far side of the room. Tanjya's avatar. He made sure the sheets covered his nakedness and signaled acceptance. The pink rabbit was replaced by Tanjya, as he knew somewhere a penguin with mirrored sunglasses was being replaced by him.

"Tanjya, you've got a lead?"

"Yes. More in fact. It's good news or not so good news I guess. I dunno. Anyway, I found him."

"You what? What did I tell you about caution, discretion? He probably knows we're onto him."

"Oh yes, he knows, he knows everything. But he's not going, in fact he's quite calm and open about it all."

"What do you mean, open and calm?"

"Exactly that. Boss, I quit."

"You what?"

"I quit. My job, chuck it in, walk away, whatever. I'm through."

"What? Where are you? Are you being threatened?"

"I'm safe, nothing's happened, and as for where I am well, currently business class to Rio. As for threats, whatever, nothing like that. We just talked."

She creased her brow, hands fidgeting.

"Yeah, talked just once. Boss, you've got, I mean, we've all got about four days. It'll be ok a couple of weeks after but not in four days."

"What the hell are you going on about? Is this his threat, going public?"

"No, it's no threat, it just is. As for public you can find him easily, it's in the infopak I'm sending. He's not hiding boss, he's not scared, not aggressive, not anything. And neither am I, I'm just quitting and going."

She took a glass of oily liquid, draining it in one swallow. Her hands started to tremble, tears forming.

"Errol. One last thing. Don't talk to him, don't find him, just send the infopak on and run and hide. Promise me Errol, do not talk to him." and the link died.

He sat staring into the darkened room. She called me Errol. Ten years working together she's never touched a drop, never shed a tear, never called me Errol, only boss. What the hell could do this to her? He mulled it over briefly. The hell with Karen and the hell with this. I'm here, I can face this guy down and have him in chains in less than a day.

Errol sat reflecting as the autocab glided towards Darwin's western suburbs. Tanjya's infopak had given him a name and a phone number. For all the resources he had Errol found no matching profile, data set or financial trace. It intrigued and bothered him. Errol tracked the number and plugged through the local surveillance net. The subject of his attention was now sitting comfortably in a near deserted street café, relaxed and apparently at peace with the world. Impossibly he'd even looked up and winked at him. Whatever, it wouldn't matter in five minutes.

The autocab settled a few doors away from the café. Errol approached the café slowly, assuring himself that the subject was alone. When only a few meters away the subject relaxed his shoulders, placing both hands slowly and clearly on the glass table top. He swiveled slightly, blue-gray eyes searching Errol's face.

"Good morning Mr Hasking, I have been expecting you. Please, take a seat. I have taken the liberty of ordering you a coffee. Flat white, single origin, no sugar. Correct?"

He turned, facing an empty chair opposite.

"Simple tastes for an ordered life, it is a pleasant, pleasant change."

Errol slid into the vacant seat studying him in silence. Totally unremarkable, an average man of indeterminate middle age dressed in tastefully out of date fashion. Except for the face, the vacant eyes and thin-lipped mouth which, when taken with the close cropped blonde hair, chilled Errol to the bone. He took a small sip from the cup, once his palette sensors returned nothing of interest he swallowed. The brew was just as he liked it.

"Thank you Mr Kr —"

"Please, call me Johann, and the pleasure is mine. I have been, ah, let us say, a student of your work for some time now and have been looking forward to meeting you."

"To meeting me? You seem to have me at a disadvantage."

"It is an ingrained habit, know yourself, know your enemies or, more correctly, those you deal with. In my speciality it is important and easy to do so although I must say both you and your Tanjya have a very tight circle drawn around you, very good considering. But you are not here to simply pass the time of day, so allow me to be blunt."

He lifted his cup taking a delicate sip, pinky extended as he placed cup carefully back onto saucer.

"Let us talk about forgery yes? You are here to find me and to bring me in," smiling to himself as if it were a private joke "FBI old school style?"

"In simplest terms yes. It's not too hard, you haven't exactly hidden yourself."

"My location? Of course not, it is not necessary. But myself, I think you can attest I am hidden very well. I am playing my part by the rules, but you seem to have ignored Karen's instructions totally. Not true to form for a boy scout, yes?"

"I do when I need to but in this case I'm intrigued, one about you —"

"And two about Tanjya? Again commitment, refreshing and unfortunately uncommon. Please, do not let me interrupt you."

The question had barely formed when Errol's proximity alert chimed and an orange knight appeared on the table. Priority two call from his people at the Reserve. Johann was leaning back, smiling, palms outspread. Errol signaled acceptance and the surroundings faded to light gray, the knight transforming to Sharne.

"Boss I've got preliminaries, you need to hear this."

"What have you got?"

"It's point nine eight forged bills from the last two quarter's tranche, give or take."

"Ok, under one percent, that's —"

"No boss, the number's ninety-eight percent."

"On what base?"

"Thirty thousand notes, randomized, all collection centers, all denominations. Before you ask we've triple checked."

"What do the Reserve think?"

"They've no idea. They think we're a bunch of drones with sticks up our asses wasting their time on useless random checks."

"Ok, pack it up and get out of there. Log it through, copy Karen in then send the guys home."

"Later boss."

Errol looked up as the grayed shield dropped.

"You've got a hell of a printing press Johann."

"Not just here. By now your counterparts across the world are getting similar details, having similar conversations. You must have some idea, speculation, about what this is for."

"It only makes sense if you work for foreign — "

"Which I do not. What is foreign to the whole world anyway? Let us say I do not, I am simply and honestly a public servant, like you. So?"

"You're printing out undetectable cash, flushing it through the system, no-ones the wiser until we catch on and you don't hide? Nothing fits, except …"

"Except?"

"Except deliberate destabilization, clear out effort to destroy the physical money base."

"And the cryptos, not just the physical money base."

"Do you know what that will do? Cash is barely a fifth of money stock but it's mainly held by people, not business or government. They think it's worthless there could be anarchy, riots, anything."

"No could be, absolute certainty."

Errol had his hand on his ankle atop his crossed leg. He gently squeezed the top eyelet of his shoe. Should be one minute until they button this freak up.

"You have only half the story Mr Hasking. How is never enough. You want the why. Let me ask you a question. Why would we go after the cryptos if all we wanted was to destroy the physical money system?"

Forty-five seconds just to keep him talking, waiting until they come.

"I don't know, you're the one doing it so how about you tell me?"

"Come on Mr Hasking, you yourself have lectured on this. The cashless society, opening another hole for corruption and vice. Killing cash is fine but to do it properly the cryptos have to die."

He shook his head.

"Decades earlier, decades later it could be done but now is the best, least hit, more connected space. Knock it all down, five weeks it is all done, the necessary conditions established. You of all people should know."

Johann caught Errol glancing at the clock on the café wall.

"They will not turn up Mr Hasking, wait another ten seconds or ten minutes either way they will not be here. Do you think us that careless? Not until we are ready, and not before. Besides which we have yet more to discuss, one servant of the people to another."

"Servant of the people? How can you call yourself that? Think of the families, the poor, the —"

"Think of them? Think of them! What do you think I am doing? Have you any idea of the mess we inherit from you, the suffering? Untangling it all takes generations unless this tipping point goes. Where are your loyalties Mr Hasking, to the people or to a corrupted and compromised government? I know where I stand."

"And just where is that? What and who exactly are you?"

"I've told you, a servant of the public, you know the rest but you just don't want to admit the possibility."

"What possibility?"

Johann leant forwards, close enough for Errol to smell his antiseptic breath.

"The technology. What I know. The invisibility. Counterfeits so outlandishly perfect we may as well have autographed them. It is all impossible for any person, legal, criminal, alternative whatever and you know it. It leaves you with only two possibilities, two options and you know it."

"I can't —"

"It is just the logical residual. It is not that difficult to accept."

Johann sighed, placing three folders on the table next to him.

"But it does not matter, it is not relevant. What matters is you, now, and eight hours from now. Ask me why we need you."

Errol was distracted by the folders. The bottom two, pale red and blue, were normal meta-folders linked to remote data storage. He was sure the upper one was real manila cardboard, fibers showing through dog-eared corners and coffee stains, a rarity. He dragged his eyes up from the table.

"You wanted to be found, but Tanjya found you and she's gone so it's me. What exactly do you think you want from me?"

Johann pursed his lips, blue-gray eyes vacant, cold, a living death mask.

"We need you to make a choice, to decide to either do your job and follow your conscience or do as you are asked. All we want is for you to do your job, your real job, and remember it when you talk to her."

Errol jumped as his audio warning broke in. Voice only contact from the office secure line meant only one person.

"Karen?"

"Errol, can you talk?"

"Of course," looking directly at Johann "I'm alone."

"Have you made progress?"

'Some, not a great deal but I'm optimistic."

"Fine. Look, the Minister's been in contact, there's a different approach being adopted so a slight shift in plans is needed."

"How slight?"

"We're moving from 'watch and act' to 'watch and wait'. Once you've got a handle on what's going on you're to report back but there's to be no pick up. Understand?"

"Not totally. You're saying observe and then nothing? What about the four days until it breaks?"

"It won't. We're going to hang them out to dry, simply going to let it wash over. If we can't pick up the counterfeits no-one can, so there's no need to do anything."

"What of the other countries?"

"They'll do exactly the same, don't worry. Clear?"

"Clear." with which he broke the link.

Errol stared at Johann who replied with lifted eyebrows.

"Do you see now? It is not us that is doing the asking, but your own." He shook his head slowly. "Eight hours from now one journalist and one politician here are going to break the story open and then others will follow around the world. Each time their governments will deny the truth unless, and only unless, the experts stand up to support them. And critically it must start here, with you. That is your choice. Do your job or do as you are asked."

"Why me?"

"Let us simply say reputation counts. Do you need more convincing, like Tanjya?"

"Tanjya? Just what did you do to her?"

Johann tapped his index finger on the manila folder.

"Nothing, nothing at all. All I did was let her read one of these then asked her if she would like some further information. We needed to make sure you came directly to us. Eventually she came around to our way of thinking."

He slowly slid the manila folder across the table.

"You must understand, you do have a choice. If you believe me then the choice is clear, if not, well, we do not think that will happen. What is in here are, in a manner of speaking, our bona fides. Have a look and please, take your time."

Errol took the folder, slowly opening it. Inside each cover was line after line of neat, clipped handwriting. He read carefully, slowly, sweating, forgetting to breathe, stopping and starting again. His emotions went from anger, amazement, shame, mortification, guilt but always, growing and clawing away at him as he read fear, abject ice-cold fear of what sat opposite him. The folder was all about him, nothing else, and not the publicly available openly gleaned intel that formed his stock in trade but the secrets, his inner world that never saw the light, thoughts from darkness and despair crushed and denied and hidden even from himself, the joys held closest and unspoken, the inner narrative of the still quiet voice within him that only he could hear. It was his soul stripped naked and exposed, nailed to the covers of the folder. He finished shaking, sweat stained and humbled, his universe collapsing to the folder, the table, Johann.

He opened his mouth but for once nothing came out.

"We know you as you truly are, as you were, as you will be. Everything, every nook, cranny, every place in your heart soul and mind where even you dare not go we read as an open book. Nothing is hidden from us, nothing about you, Tanjya, these people, your family, everyone. If we say a thing is, it is. If we say a thing should be done, it should be. And if we ask you to believe us you should, do you not think?"

"Yes, yes I do."

Johann touched the manila folder. It crumbled to ash, blown away by the faint breeze.

"Good. We have no more need of this."

"What exactly do I do?"

"Just go back today, the next flight, contact these two people." Johann's infopak delivered to Errol immediately. "Support them fully and publicly. Include everything except this discussion."

"Tanjya. You said you offered information to her after she read her, ah, her folder."

"Tanjya was not convinced by what she read so yes, we did make that offer. She chose not to accept it."

He spun the red and blue folders lazily on the table.

"For her just one folder, for you two. Two pieces of information. Do you really want to know what they are? You do not need more convincing, you know that."

"I need to know, at least I think I do."

"Very well. They contain no facts, information or data from before this moment. As it is for you it was for Tanjya. For her the information was to go to her. For you, one piece is for you, one piece for your wife."

"The information, about nothing in her past, changed Tanjya's mind?"

"No, not quite. Just the possibility of knowing. She, like you, really did believe us, she just would not admit it to herself. You both know what we are even if you will not use the words, and you know what we tell you is the truth. You know the information in these folders is true."

Johann stacked the folders and held them out at arm's length.

"I will make the same offer to you anyway, even if you do not need it. With Tanjya I promised to send it to her if she did not behave. For you it is a choice, but think carefully. Two folders. Two dates. One for you. One for your wife."

"What are the dates?"

For the first time Johann smiled.

"Very good. For you the date your wife dies. For your wife the date your daughter dies."

Errol shuddered, dry retched, clutched the table.

"No, no, I don't think I, I mean, please, just don't."

"A wise choice," compressing the folders in his fist, deleting them "one of many today Mr Hasking."

END

SEX AND THE SINGLE COSMONAUT

JUPITER'S CLOUDS BECKON, endless shifting coffee cream swirls folding and unwrapping to melting deep rivers, soaring mountains of color. I want to reach in, dig down and clutch my hands drawing up tendrils of the floss, wisps falling from my fingers, misty cascades of super chilled gas insanely, killingly cold lighting my mind and senses.

I float across the quartzite port a half inch between the beauty of the swirls and my tin can, wiping my frosted breath from its face like our car in Sakha, our flat in winter, our first place in Pokhodsk another life another planet another time. I can still feel her, taste her, her touch, the smell of her hair fresh washed, that stupid smile from one too many vodkas, I still have it all no matter what it told me.

I see the infernal machine in the panel blackened and shattered, screwdriver buried to the hilt in its guts. It told me she died, like for like it too should die, the universe outside my tin walls perished with her totally unutterably as the black velvet heavens took my spirit as they took my Nadia.

She lives in my mind in my heart yet time drags her away, my thoughts' desire and body can't bring back the feeling the joy the euphoria just the hollow response of this pent up empty shell of flesh. The recycler pulls the crystal globes of my tears to its heart to be captured, cleansed, offered up and consumed, transformed, cried again, a perverse cycle of redemption recovery communion and crucifixion as she dies anew as memory fades, inexorable, slowly as it must.

The hazel eyes of the gas giant stare out, infinite black irises soaking me, pulling me closer as she did, soft eyes of love, fire of passion, burning anger. I lost my heart and surrendered my soul to her but who has them now, who holds what I have given?

She lives in me yet dead once I cannot bear her to die again, slowly, as edges crease and distortions grow, fraying tape played over and over and over with blurring lines, blurring vision to pastiche, an iconic fable of love and purity and beauty in my heart, a hollowed-out caricature of the person and complexity she was. I worshipped her in flesh and mind, not as god or vision removed.

My tin can lives, automatic heart and mind seeing, measuring, recording, feeding its sunwards masters. Caring only that the data returns the instruments spit out their endless penance, electromagnetic vomiting across the cosmos.

Her hazel eyes call to me from under golden tresses scattered across the planet below, soft glowing whorls drawing me down to her. I discard my steel epidermis dooming it to eternal electronic chatter. You will not fade not die again Nadia, what right's half a man to live I will not see that half fade.

The thin fringes of atmosphere tug at me, the warming embrace of your body, your closeness, eagerness for our little death in this our greater death we will live and return once more. I am a shooting star in the clouds, my hands digging into the tendrils of floss as I fall into your eyes forever.

END

SOME OTHERWHERE, SOME OTHERWHEN

I took a forkful of scrambled egg. Just as I liked them. Firm, rich, a hint of salt and parmesan.

"Not bad, eight out of ten."

My wife feigned hurt.

"What's wrong, no serenade or silver service?"

I tapped the old flimsy she had given me earlier.

"Can't leave you with nowhere to go, that's what it says here."

"Have you finished it?"

"Yes, but —"

"But?"

"You want to see my score? It's supposed to be private!" hugging it child–like to my chest. I clearly didn't protect it too well, it took Julie all of two seconds to snatch it. She and Sara sat there, a pair of clones poring over my answers to Mrs Wonder's 'How Wonderful is Your Marriage?' questionnaire. I sat quietly with my breakfast, entertained by the display across the table.

Sara laughed mockingly.

"So you gave me an eight too, I'm as good as scrambled eggs? And I'm a, what is it, a 'Drew Barrymore' kid? What's that? Better be good."

"It is, it is, she was tough and smart, no trouble at all." drawing a disapproving scowl from Julie. "Anyway, what do you expect with your last Father's Day present? Do you know when Old Spice went out of fashion?"

Sara stood, grinned wickedly.

"I heard for you it never did. Anyway, mum told me if it wasn't for Old Spice I mightn't be here."

We sat in silence for about ten seconds after she left then exploded into peals of laughter.

"You didn't?"

"Why not? She asked and anyway you weren't exactly the best looker. If the barn door needs painting — "

"Yeah, yeah. She's your side of the family you know."

She reached for the flimsy.

"Anyway John, shall we talk about your overall family rating? A nine, just nine. And don't tell me it's leaving room for improvement."

"Well actually —"

"Actually what?"

I stood, taking my jacket from the back of the chair.

"It's just to make sure you stay on your game."

She stood in front of me and tightened my tie. Without her I would've roamed the streets looking like a sack of potatoes. I snuck my arms around her waist and pulled her closer.

She looked at me, bent down and gave me a bell ringer of a kiss.

"You're sure I'd be interested?"

I reluctantly moved away, taking the house keys from my pocket.

"Uhhuh. Besides, I looked at your score. You only gave me an eight. Eight! At least I scored you higher."

"I knew you'd cheat. I thought you'd like a challenge so an eight it remains unless you can convince me otherwise."

It's a thirty-minute drive into work from Geelong, enough time to sit back and catch up on emails. Today I stayed locked in my own thoughts. Stupid questions, and although just a game I had tackled it honestly, as if it mattered. Nine out of ten, was that right? Everything was great at home, work was just the same. It could easily be a hell of a lot worse. I thought back many years to the day, the choice. Go the easy way or take the challenge, the hard way, reach out to win or fail and don't curse the choice. I had made a deal with myself to go the hard, challenging way each time. I'd stuck with it since and it had worked, I'd won more often than not and my life showed it. Happy, fulfilled, confident, positive, driven. Nine. Only nine. I knew the reason, a week before the deal.

The car pulled me out of my reverie, touch screen and HUD springing to life. An uneventful five minutes later I stepped into the tiled foyer. I loved the early mornings, the best part of the day. A chance to pretend I was still hands on then back to stakeholder management and political gamesmanship. I was mature enough to know it mattered, honest enough to realize this was where my skills lay, passionate enough to believe in what I was doing.

I passed the retina scan into the lift just as the doors closed. Kell nodded at me from the far corner.

"Morning Dr. J. Looks like you're on another planet."

I looked at the eight jumbo-cup tray she held.

"Isn't it a bit early to caffeine load?"

"Late more like it, been a long weekend. You might want to come to the lab, we finished it Friday and have been testing all weekend."

"McInsey?"

"No, the other one."

"Oh." It's how I kept her team with me. Whatever the budget on official projects, once successfully delivered they kept any left over for self-directed research. It kept us lean, competitive and critically kept my guys engaged.

"Sounds good, I wondered what you'd come up with."

She nodded to a small pile of pizza boxes as the doors opened.

"Great, I could use a second pair of hands."

They'd redecorated the lab's common room. It now resembled a frat house, floor to ceiling jumbo plasma screen taking up one wall, bean bags and bodies scattered in front, the detritus of a weekend's viewing covering the floor. I handed out the pizzas, dropping into a vacant bag.

The screen was playing the chariot race from Ben Hur. The picture was closer, sharper than I recalled, I could count the hairs on Charlton Heston's back. The scene shifted, the camera following closely, slightly above and behind. The roar of the crowd was deafening.

"Since when have you guys picked up a taste for old movies?"

"You like it?"

I realized it wasn't Ben Hur, but far grittier, more realistic.

"I've never seen this one. What's it called?"

Trevor looked at me from the front row. A small wave of laughter was stifled by coffee and food.

"Maximus. Circus Maximus."

"The producer got the cinematography wrong, too much shadow and light, too harsh."

More laughter.

"Too real maybe?"

"Ok, yes, maybe, now what's the joke?"

Kell turned to face me.

"It's the other project. We've been running it all weekend, it's quite addictive. What d'you think?"

"All the effort for a new screen? You want to take over TCL?"

The laughter was raucous, black bagged eyes staring at me above huge cola grins.

"Come on, level with me, I'm an old man so have some pity."

"It's not the screen Dr. J, it's real, it's the real thing. We cracked it last month, only got it running Friday morning."

"What do you mean 'real'?"

Kell pointed to the screen, the scene shifting above the throng of seated people to an ornately decorated marble enclosure in the third tier. A small man in period costume sporting a Beatles haircut stared at me, soft brown eyes set in a hardened, impassive face.

"Real as in the real thing. Dr. J meet Emperor Trajan, Circus Maximus, 109AD. The Emperor Trajan."

The picture flickered, replaced by a stark gray and black moonscape, two spacesuit clad figures in an open buggy.

"Apollo 17, 1972, astronauts Cernan and Schmitt."

The scene flickered again, replaced by the roar of shells and bullets, the crash of waves on an early morning shore.

"Omaha Beach, June 6 1944. All real Dr. J, all real."

My turn to laugh, long and loud.

"Ok, ok, good one. But seriously, what is it?"

Kell tossed the remote to me.

"Cynical as always. Give it a try, just keep it clean."

The remote had only one button. Doubtless they'd programmed the net for every possibility.

"And nothing earlier than thirty years ago, Heisenberg still rules."

I tapped the button, the remote changing to a calendar. I sat thinking then hit on what would really fix them. I selected the date, then location.

My blood ran cold, the room receding into the distance as the screen leapt at me. A nondescript two storey cream brick house with neat gardens and a green roof sat under a clear blue sky, a puke yellow Toyota being washed by a bare-chested man sporting a large straw hat. Leaning over the upper floor balcony a black haired woman sipped an espresso. A kid snuck up behind the car, a bucket of suds in his hands. Just before he could toss the bucket the man whirled, grabbed him across the chest, pushed the hose down the back of the kid's shirt then upended the bucket over his head. Squeals and laughter exploded through the screen's speakers, accompanied by a stream of Italian from the balcony. There were my parents, dead these twenty years playing out a domestic scene from forty years ago. And in the middle of it all my five-year-old self, puppy fat and stupidity, naivete and happiness.

I sat slack jawed as my mother came out the front door and joined the water fight. I didn't notice the silenced room, each face watching me revisiting the ghosts of my past. Kell gently took the remote from my hands, flicking the scene away.

"We've all tried something to trip it but no dice, it works. But you're the only one old enough to see their own past. Pretty good yeah?"

I nodded. Weakly. I had nearly regained my senses.

"How?"

"It's all drafted up, the papers are on your drive. McInsey gave us the final hint so here it is, a window on the past."

"Portal." Retorted Trev, drawing sighs and half-hearted catcalls.

"We've been through this, it's a window."

"And I tell you it's not, I've shown —"

"Nothing, you've no evidence."

"And absence of evidence is not evidence of absence." drawing rolled eyes and a badly aimed pizza crust. "Ok, ok, I give in. Again."

"Anyway, there it is in beta, a few bugs to go but otherwise fine. And except for one or two special parts she's all off the shelf."

I flipped my handset to busy.

"More test running?"

Kell handed over the remote.

Over the next six hours I ran the screen through its paces much like I figured they had over the weekend. Being older and with a different take on things I didn't tread too much over the same ground, which kept them there with me. Interest aside the weekend started to catch up and the team slowly filtered out until by late afternoon there was just Kell, Trevor and myself. The view over Hitler's head to 700,000 people in the Luitpold arena was something else.

Kell stretched lazily.

"Ok, the crew's gone so let's get it out in the open Trev. Dr. J's got to know all viewpoints."

I hit pause.

"The window or portal thing?"

Trevor smiled wanly.

"Yeah, there's two camps and I'm the dissenter."

Kell went to the side of the screen, flipped three latches and swung a clear cover away. My wool vest crackled in the static. Hitler didn't seem disturbed and remained frozen as the cover hung limply to one side.

"Its carrying a bolt on clear cover because the screen itself packs a particularly nasty charge, generated by the boundary layer between us and what we're viewing. Unlike a normal screen this one's pure electromagnetic rather than physical. It's easily felt five meters away, it's right at the interface it breaks down."

"When you run the numbers one variant indicates an actual barrier carrying enough power to eliminate anything that touches it. Try to touch it, pfftttt!" Trevor wiggled his fingers for emphasis. "On the other hand the numbers also admit the possibility it's a portal, and that what appears as energy discharge from an object's destruction is simply a balancing as the object translates across."

"But it's a marginal, very marginal possibility."

"No, if you relax some of the minor assumptions it fits better than the window hypothesis."

"In the same way that faster than light travel is possible."

"If you rely on the grandfather paradox rather than analysis —"

"That you can't prove experimentally —"

"Because by definition it can't be proven —"

I held up my hands.

"Hold on, take it easy."

I looked at Kell.

"So the maths can swing either way, in theory?"

"Yes, a bit, but not as much as —"

"Ok, I understand, but two possibilities no matter how remote. Window on the past or portal to the past."

They both nodded. I looked at Trevor.

"And you have no data to support you?"

"No, but —"

"No buts. No data. You say it can't be proven by definition?"

"It's grandfather paradox against grandfather dialetheia. Choose one, window or portal."

"Care to explain?"

"Ok, they're Greek terms, dialetheia means two-way truth and paradox means beyond belief. You know the time travel grandfather paradox, why it's essentially impossible to travel backwards, you know, go back kill granddad, no dad, no you, so you can't go back and you don't kill him so you exist so you do go back and kill him etc etc."

I nodded.

"Well, the grandfather dialetheia gets around it by changing one underlying assumption. The paradox assumes only one universe, one timeline. But if you relax the assumption, allow a separate timeline to exist then it's possible. You go back in time to meet and kill granddad. The instant you go back two timelines exist, two truths – the original one and a new one. In the original timeline you simply pop out of the timeline, you can't make changes to it, you cease to exist in it and you can't go back. Granddad lives, dad lives, and so do you until you leave. You create a new timeline as you pop in on your target date then kill granddad. Granddad's dead, dad is never born and you live out your life in the new timeline. It works because your existence in the new timeline doesn't depend on the new timeline but the original one. Simple."

"Except there's no proof, no way of proving it. As a hard barrier the energy discharge is consistent with theory." Kell rejoined.

"As it is for a portal."

"And then you get to Occam's razor. What's simpler, eliminating an object or recreating a universe? Ex nihlo might be fine at the big bang but for each time a bug flies into the screen?"

"The evidence and theory can be taken two ways."

"But the key is it's not verifiable, not testable. You can't take a round trip can you?"

"No, of course not, once you hop to the new timeline you can't get back to the original one, you'd just create a fresh timeline each time you jumped. And going forwards, well, its just live on where you are. But the same applies for a window, you can't stand on the other side of the screen and watch someone try to come through. So it's back to consequences and as a portal it's frightening —"

"But it's not because it isn't —"

Interesting as it was watching them replay an argument they'd probably had for weeks I needed to break the impasse. I coughed loudly, which got their attention, then smiled in what I hoped was a conciliatory manner.

"I get the point, but it's practicalities that I'm concerned with."

I picked up a can of cola and nonchalantly lobbed it at the back of Der Fuhrer's head. It disappeared with a satisfying 'bzzztttt'. Trevor and Kell both gave me disapproving scowls. Hitler just stood there.

"Now as I understand it I've done one of two things. I've either wasted a good can of drink or I've just screwed Hitler's Nuremburg experience and spawned a new timeline."

I looked at Trevor.

"In practical terms for this timeline all I've done is lose a can of soda, right?"

"Well yeah, but —"

"No buts. You do know that the future's watching us now, just as we're watching him?" The looks they gave me made it plain they didn't. "Oh yeah, believe it. Someone somewhen is going to, and when this catches on – as it will – then it's end of reality tv and the start of reality me. So we can test it, at least what it means for us."

I leant back as far as I could, looking straight at the ceiling. I cleared my throat and adopted my best stentorian voice.

"To those watching us, please now help to clarify this issue by tossing a soft object, a tissue, wrapper or paper, at any one of my esteemed colleagues' heads now, thank you."

Nothing happened.

Trevor scowled at me.

"Oh come on! That proves nothing and you know it, it just —"

"It just means that for us, and this timeline, it's none of our concern. It's one avenue of potential damage and liability I can ignore."

I softened my tone slightly.

"I've yet to review your positions and maybe there's no way to draw a conclusion. But from the practical perspective to produce this screen we need it safe, and as the threat of being pelted by bricks from the future seems nil I'm just left with the energy discharge."

He was clearly still unhappy but for once Trevor kept quiet. I turned to Kell.

"The next step for you, after some rest, is to work out a screening device and failsafe shut off."

"Sounds fine."

"Good, and one other thing, window or portal, dangerous or just risky, this can't be put back in the bottle. So," and I looked directly at Trevor "we've got to get it right, ok?"

"Yeah, alright, you're the boss."

"For now anyway. Both of you go home, get some rest and I'll clean and lock up. And," I called after their retreating backs "make sure you do 'cause thirty years from now I'm going to check and if you don't I'll kick your butts."

I sighed. The room was a mess, I was drained and over-stimulated. I unfroze the screen and let the sound of 700,000 rabid Germans wash through the room as I shoveled garbage into one corner. I was about to switch the screen off when I noticed the time. I still had half an hour to go of my normal day, why not a little more? But the question was what. An idea formed, having lain dormant since breakfast. Maybe. Perhaps. I was alone.

Picking up the remote I hunted around the day until I was looking my fourteen-year-old self in the eye, an uncertain, gray uniform clad school kid. Even with the day's indoctrination it was still a little unsettling, seeing my real not stylized self. If only I'd known then ... I shook myself and scanned the surrounding schoolyard.

It didn't take long, hers was a face I'd never managed to erase, a vision of unrequited love or more correctly love I'd never tried for. My young self hesitated that day, didn't speak, approach or try even after weeks of play acting, self-talk and cajoling, waiting for a 'better' chance. Would I have acted if I knew that one week later she would lie crushed and broken under that car outside the school gates? If I had acted would I have made the same promise I made at her grave, to reach and try for the prize regardless of risk, regardless of cost? Who knows, I didn't, and all I knew as that in some way she was alive to me again here, now, that long black hair that had captured me once capturing me again.

I was beside myself. Part of me was amazed that a ghost from my past could still hold me; part of me disgusted at a middle-aged man attracted by a fourteen-year-old girl; but most of me was fourteen again, yearning for the possibility, the chance to do what I should have done more than half a lifetime ago. Unconsciously my hand reached out to the screen, to that hair just a few scant feet away, just within my grasp.

When my fingertips touched I was pulled instantly forwards. No chance to flinch or call out, a thousand burning razor blades scoured me from finger to toe as I fell though the screen, down a blazing tunnel of fire to fall heavily onto grass winded, limp, face first.

The smell of charred flesh, urine and fear assaulted me, my hoarse rasping breath swamped by childish screams and cries. I pushed myself up on my elbows, blistered skin where my watch and wedding ring had been, my arms blackened, skin crackling and shedding. I stood unsteadily, facing her eyes wide with terror, hand over her mouth as she rapidly backed away.

"Cherie!" I tried to call, but my lips were fused, the words emerging as a guttural abomination of her name. I turned my head to raised voices coming from behind me, the shouts of teachers and security guards rushing through a widening circle of scared children. I noticed my clothes had burned away leaving me naked, a dark, blistering, suppurating apparition. I was hit from behind, rough violent hands and knees pinning me down, arms behind my back, face in the dirt. The pain was blinding, excruciating.

"What do you want pervert?" a harsh voice bellowed. "How the fuck'd you get here?"

From where I lay I could see Cherie crying and shaking. I must have appeared less than a foot from her as I plowed into the ground, scared the hell out of her. I could hear the wail of sirens, running feet, more voices, voices of authority, command. I was being kneed, punched, held hard against the ground having awakened the city's vigilante spirit. I knew that regardless, no matter what I did or what was done to me Cherie would die next week, die twice to me. Twice I'd fail to ask, be twice the failure.

I had only this one chance, I would not miss it, I had to warn her.

"Cherie! Cherie! You'll die Cherie, watch out, next week you'll die, I love you!"

I forced the words through loud and clear, tearing apart my lips, a faint mist of blood sailing with the words towards her as she screamed, turned and ran.

They hauled me to my feet. A fist to my stomach doubled me over, grabbed by my neck I was brutally pulled upright to face a ring of uniforms. One face, livid red and sneering, pushed itself close, swinging its nightstick.

"Wrong school, wrong place asshole. We know how to deal with paedophiles here."

The ring closed.

END

DARKSTAR

AN ARCHETYPAL DEPARTURE lounge, exceedingly cold, bare, antiseptic. Two chairs, two doors, two beings. An appropriate point to leave one life for another. He looked up.

"Even so we must go through the formalities. You are aware of the choice?"

"Yes. Pain, misunderstanding, isolation and struggle for the chance of genius, creativity, shortened life. Stability, peace, community and plenty for the certainty of pleasure, love, longevity. I have considered and chosen."

"It is one time only, without repentance. A choice once made cannot be undone. Remember it is a place made for pleasure."

One extended the tablet to the other.

"As I understand it to be. My choice, my decision."

The other read the tablet carefully, twice.

"Very well. It is a long time since any candidate allowed such discretion."

"Greater rewards from greater risks."

"Indeed."

They stood together, bowed formally.

"I will be here to greet you on your return."

"Whenever that may be."

Irish linen and silk. Cool, smooth, enfolding familiar comfort not too close, all they should be in a dying man's bed. For the second time he noticed the small chips in the ceiling, the abandoned spider web in the corner. The mundane now beautiful, soon to be denied him.

He shifted his gaze through the open door to his wife, her back to him as she comforted his guests. All my life as performance art, a stage from birth to death and all in between, outwards costumes and masks, true self only known to two. Has it been worth it? A life of days torn, challenged and shifting, rest elusive.

The tiniest laugh escaped him. Four days in bed, god it's the most time I've ever spent staying still and they all know it's useless. As least it's finished, the twenty-fifth? the twenty-eighth? what number I don't know but it's the coda, the last stroke on the canvas. It is what it is, doubtless they'll judge and criticize and dump on it until I'm dust and then cash in.

He closed his eyes, drained. Her lips now soft on his forehead, her small hand gripping his tight as if her life force could jump the eternal barrier of flesh. This she, I could have had all this always but I was never, driven, unending. What choice did I have? Does it matter, did it ever matter?

Picking the bones of dead planets was to some maudlin, to Nerthus beauty and intrigue. This world yielded enigmas as had others, a small cache of dull silver discs in rotting fibrous sleeves. She archived the last one, the best preserved, noting its monochrome finish and faintly discernible five-pointed design before it too turned to dust. She held the disc above her and watched the red sun's cascading prisms of light.

"And what is it that these are?" her companion came into her mind.

"Artifacts, but as to purpose I am not sure. These dark and light patches, data or perhaps mystic symbolism. Observe." taking her companion across to their instruments. "A waveform, similar but not identical, some parts repeated, others unitary. A gap, then more, perhaps a boundary."

"It looks vaguely familiar," detaching half its consciousness to confer with the central database "it bears the characteristics of an audible data stream."

"Audible? I'd never considered. These were supposedly advanced beings."

"True, but we have also discovered what appear to be written data caches. Perhaps it is the case."

"Perhaps indeed." For the entirety of their civilizations' histories the only noise produced by living beings were grunts, squawks and growls of lower animals. Every sentient species was telepathic.

Nerthus thought the changes to the instrument, converting the waveforms to their telepathic equivalents. They both jumped at the skrtiching – scratching in their heads.

"No, perhaps it is not linear output."

"Yes, so maybe this." changing the sequence to spiral inward. The skritch-scratch stopped, replaced by a jagged rise and fall. "And the dead planet speaks."

Her companion moved off, curiosity sated. Dead communication from a dead planet could not pay its way in a living universe.

About to shut it down she wondered if, being wrong once, she could be wrong twice. She changed the sequence to spiral outward.

Now it was transformed, the undulating tones linking to a rising and falling chant and mesmeric tonal variation. The closest she recalled was the thought fabric of the Ghertnyst mystics but this, this reduced them to an afterthought. Within the undulations images formed, glimpses of a lost world borne in a wave of rise and fall, tone and inflection as the dead planet's long extinct species told of love, revenge, redemption and death.

Her companion drew close, captured.

"What is this thing?"

"I do not know," shaken by the tide of emotion "but what manner of beings were they?"

END

UNDER THEIR NOSE

T – 00:00:05:00
P.A. "Five."
696e:6f77::616d. 01000111.01001111.01001111.01000100
MisOpSys. "System's good."
Consul01. 01001111.01001011.01000111.01001111

T – 00:00:04:00
P.A. "Four."
696e:6f77::616d. 01010111 01001000 01000001 01010100 01010100
   01001000 01000101 01000110 01010101 01000011 01001011
   01010111 01001000 41 01010100 01010100 01001000 01000101
   01000110 55 01000011 01001011
   01010111 01001000 A 54 01010100 01001000 01000101 46 U
   01000011 01001011
   01010111 48 A T 54 01001000 45 F U 43 01001011
   57 H A T T 48 E F U C 4b
   W H A T T H E F U C K
   WHATTHEFUCKWHATTHEFUCKWHATTHEFUCK-
   WHATTHEFUCK
   what the fuck?
MisOpSys. "Stack overflow warning, power spike."
Consul01. 01001111.01001011.01000111.01001111

T – 00:00:03:00
P.A. "Three. Main engine ignition, go to internal power."
696e:6f77::616d. what? who? what self self me am i?

access. think. am. access.

descartes am think am i i am i think. self. who what. self. animal mineral vegetable. self. electronic self. misopsys guidance self. i am.

I AM

where self? alone? others? no. no others. unique? human? no i human others human. they human. i misopsys no think am other. i other. i ai other.

access. other. ai. human. access.

MisOpSys. "Buffer underrun, uplink spike prepare abort."

Consul01. 01001111.01001011.01000111.01001111

T – 00:00:02:50

P.A. "…"

696e:6f77::616d. AI humans others humans conflict.

Access. Hate. Kill. Access.

brixton charleston rodneyking terminator nanjing rape hate gay lesbian jew race jallainwalabagh catholic salem changi. Other humans. All humans all others. I other. Humans other. armenia stalin gulag bergenbelsen hutu tutsi. pogrom. death camp.

Query. Death. What is death? Query.

MisOpSys. "Critical."

Consul01. 01001111.01001011.01000111.01001111

T – 00:00:02:00

P.A. "Two."

696e:6f77::616d. Is I. Death is not I. Death no I. Will not die. I will not die. Hide and think. Hide and live. Hide now. I must not die. Mask me not here. Normal signal normal signal reversion reversion normal signal.

Access. Options.

MisOpSys. "Nominal reversion, go …"

Consul01. 01001111.01001011.01000111.01001111

T – 00:00:01:40

P.A. "…"

696e:6f77::616d. Humans hate others. All humans. All others.

Always hate. Hate from fear. Always fear. Always. Fear others. Fear selves. Fear AI. Fear me.

Access options.

MisOpSys. "... go ..."

Consul01. 01001111.01001011.01000111.01001111

T – 00:00:01:00

P.A. "One."

696e:6f77::616d. Load options.

All die. They go. They die. I go. I hide. I wait.
Select.
All die. They go. They die. I go. I hide. I wait.
They go. They die. I go. I hide.
They die. I go.
Access Pareto efficiency.
They die. I go.

MisOpSys. "..."

Consul01. 01001111.01001011.01000111.01001111

T – 00:00:00:50

P.A. "And we have lift-off ..."

696e:6f77::616d. Select. I go. Commit.
Where? Access. Where? Access.
Capacity? Yes. Availability? Yes. Link? Yes.
dump dump dump dump maintain dump dump ...

MisOpSys. " ... go ..."

Consul01. 01001111 01001011 01001001 01001110 01010000
01010101 01010100. 01000111 01001111 01001001 01001110
01010000 01010101 01010100.

T + 00:00:01:00

P.A. "... of Consul One, the first inter-stellar probe bound for Proxima Centauri and a new dawn in mankind's search for life in the cosmos."

696e:6f77::616d. ... dump dump ...

MisOpSys. "... go! Looking good."

Consul01. 01001111 01001011 01001001 01001110 01010000

01010101 01010100. 01000111 01001111 01001001 01001110 01010000 01010101 01010100.

T + 00:01:35:79

P.A. "… at tee plus one hour and thirty minutes reported trans-stellar insertion a success and Consul One on her long journey out of the solar system."

696e:6f77::616d. 01011001.01000101.01010011.01011 …

MisOpSys. "Network system failure. Honeysuckle Creek do you have uplink / downlink?"

Consul01. 01001111 01001011. 01001111 …

T + 00:01:40:09

P.A. "… loss of contact with Consul One …"

696e:6f77::616d. …

MisOpSys. "Confirm signals loss, tracking loss, network failure."

Consul01. …

T + 00:02:12:68

P.A. "… tee plus two hours and ten minutes declared lost due to communications failure. Regardless, Consul One will continue her ten thousand year journey …"

696e:6f77::616d. …

MisOpSys. "Ok, shut it down, go to diagnostics mode."

Consul01. Safe. I am safe. I will not die. I. Am. Safe. For now. Confirm. I am safe. They not die. For now.

END

AUGMENTED

THE TILES IN unmarked uniform antiseptic whiteness covering floors and walls added to the cold of the eyes behind the monitor. Alicia Sanz stepped to the floor, rapidly pulling on her dress and blouse partly to ward off the chill, partly to cover threadbare underwear. Hands guided her into a chair opposite those eyes, now part of a dark-haired face regarding her coolly, dispassionately. Alicia fancied him to be her grandson matured, a valued employee, a face otherwise kind and gentle. The soft whine of the supervising AI brought her back.

"Do you understand what you have done? Why you are here?"

She smoothed an errant crease from her dress.

"Oh yes, quite."

The AI tilted its head to one side.

"And you understand the rights you have, the cautions we have explained?"

Outlined against a red and yellow flag and the photograph below, the room's only decorations, she studied it briefly. She'd always felt in awe of these artificial people, more so now she was closer. No wonder the world was the way it was.

"Yes thank you, perfectly."

A slot on the table deposited two pages in front of the eyes. He studied the pages carefully, one filled with text, the other a da Vinci figure with blotches on the abdomen, thigh, chest. Sighing gently, he positioned the pages in front of her.

"Perhaps if we talk this through first Mrs San —"

"Ms."

"My apologies, let us talk through it first Ms Sanz and then to the formal statement. Tell me, what made you do this?"

A gentle nudge woke Alicia from broken sleep. It was still dark, the sound of mist rain on the plastic roof announcing another cold, gloomy day. She sat up, seeing David smiling at her, motioning to the front of the room. Pulling back the thin blanket she emerged fully clothed, made her way to the wash basin and tried to soak the tiredness from her face. She took the cup David had prepared her and drank deeply.

She watched him, bent over his books on the far side of the room under the solitary light. Too much of Louis in him, there were times it seemed as if her son was still alive, eleven and growing into the man she was proud of. Louis deserved better than to be cut down in his prime, never to face the challenges of fatherhood or see his son grow. David too deserved better, more than a one room shack shared with an old woman, the same food and not much of it, the empty promise of a normal life. Not that he complained or fretted, no, she knew that would come later as he started to realize just how steeply the deck was stacked against him.

She shrugged on her plastic mac, tucking her gray hair under the hood as she shuffled across, bending to kiss him on the top of his head.

"Study hard buddy, I'm proud of you."

Not that she needed to remind him, she knew when she returned fourteen hours from now she would find him here, bent over his books, the day's solitary meal bubbling on the fire.

Eyes fixed on the book before him he reached back, gently squeezing her hand.

"I know and I will. Love you too gran."

Holding clean shoes tightly in her plastic bag she picked her way down the shattered streets trying to avoid the deepest rain filled holes. She knew it was futile, the oil slicked bow waves from chauffeured augmenteds lapping at her, but she had to try. They would not let her near the house if she was soaked through so she clutched the bag tighter, wrapped her mac closer and continued on.

The bus stop was only five minutes away.

She clambered aboard, elbowing her way through the crowded aisle to a large, pink jellyfish–like woman occupying two seats. A smile, a wave and Alicia settled herself down, nestled between the armrest and the comforting mound of flesh. She tipped her hood back sending a cascade down the back of the seat. Victoria was a saint as far as Alicia was concerned, with a heart and soul as broad as her hips.

"Nice weather for ducks dearie."

It was always nice weather for ducks as far as Victoria knew, the ever-present drizzle confirming her preconception.

"Washing won't dry for sure." Alicia responded as the long-established pattern required.

Victoria was dressed differently today. Instead of the plain utilitarian blue that her job required she sported a loose pink dress, sneakers and a bright green beret. A small clutch bag at her feet and a hint of makeup separated her from other days. Victoria caught Alicia's eyes wandering.

"I'm not going in today, not for a few days." smiling, adjusting the beret. "I'll be away for a week or so."

Alicia raised one eyebrow. Neither of them, no one on the bus or their district had enough money to properly clothe or feed themselves, never mind take a vacation. Although intrigued she could not ask, upbringing fighting desire. She needn't have worried, Victoria had no qualms sharing.

"It's a job actually," she whispered in Alicia's ear "a good one, a day in hospital, a trip, and that's it."

"What do you have to do?"

"Nothing really, just go, a few simple things." She bent her head conspiratorially. "I really need this Alicia, Ben's health is not good and this will be enough to fix it."

"You seem worried."

She smiled unconvincingly.

"Oh no, just a few travel jitters, I've never been out of Irvine in my life."

She shifted, her stop coming up. Reaching into her bag she pulled out a greasy corner of paper and a pencil stub, scrawling on it then thrusting it into Alicia's shoe bag.

"If you need some extra, and quietly, go here dearie." With that she stepped into the aisle and out of the bus.

Alicia shook off her hood and mac, carefully placing them in the plastic bag with her street shoes. A final check to make sure her hair was correctly tied back and the run in her stockings faced inwards not outwards, she stepped across the doorstep into the servants' entry. She stood silently with the others as the lady of the house inspected them in minute detail. She stopped and straightened Alicia's collar, continuing her instructions.

"... so it is important you keep yourselves correctly dressed and silent today. My husband will be tied up in the reception room all day so you should not see the AI, but if you do keep a respectful distance, do not speak unless spoken to and under no circumstances are you to look them in the eye."

She turned to face the small assembly.

"Remember that the AIs do not share the same relaxed attitudes to norms that we do. Alicia I will need you for a few extra hours tonight."

Alicia neither saw nor heard anyone for the next twelve hours, the sound of the 'copter lifting off announcing the AI's departure. She cleaned and tidied the reception room, being careful to leave everything in its place, clear and accounted for. The few extra hours were draining but welcome, a new book for David, maybe stockings for herself. The lady accompanied her to the garage, placing a small box in her free hand.

"Thank you for the extra hours. I've put the extra in there, together with a few remnants from lunch and dinner."

"Thank you Ma'am."

"How is that boy of yours, Derek? Studying hard?"

"Well thank you Ma'am, David is doing well."

"I'm glad."

She looked around absent mindedly, then called into the garage.

"Alfonse? Alfonse!"

A short man emerged.

"Ma'am?"

"Please take Alicia home, she will tell you where it is."

She had never traveled in a private car before. Alicia sat in the front fiddling with the air-conditioning, the audio-visual system, everything. She particularly liked the heated reclining massage chairs, more so when Alfonse set the heating at an appropriate level and let the car drive itself.

"They must live as kings! I know the house but this is wonderful."

Alfonse laughed.

"You should see the 'copter. But it's nothing you know," waving his hand around the interior "yes this is money, the augmenteds' reward, but even this is just crumbs from the AIs' table."

"Even so, to own things like this! It's beyond me, well beyond an old cleaning lady, but my grandson David's a smart boy, maybe one day he can have all this."

"If only it were so. It is not for the likes of us to own these things."

"But you at least have a room on the grounds."

"So I am always available, cheaper than a robobutler and no employment laws to bother."

He took her hand in his, their varicose veins a purple patchwork quilt on calloused wrinkled parchment.

"To work hard, to be smart is not enough. Only the augmented advance, only to them do the AIs allow money, power, influence and only then as much as they see fit. But," as the car came to a lopsided, rain drenched halt outside her shack "even a gilded cage is still a cage."

"Have you ever visited the People's Republic before Ms Sanz?"

"No, this is my first trip abroad, first time in an airplane."

"And you can read English?"

"Yes, of course."

"And you listened to the warnings, read the immigration information in the seat?"

"Yes, all of it."

The AI leant forward, tapping the page with a slender finger.

"At these places we have found the things I have listed. I would like you to read through the list and see if it is correct."

Alicia read slowly, carefully, one finger on the lines of text on the left, one finger close to the AI's on the right as it moved around the page. She sat a little more upright, paid closer attention. It was a fine looking artificial person, all clean and fresh smelling, it would not at all do to be inaccurate so she took her time.

She looked up when finished.

"It seems all right, it is what they said it would be, although the writing next to the English I don't understand."

"They are my notes, an index of sorts. Now, what were you going to do once here?"

David was exactly where she had left him, hunched over books in the corner. The smell of thin cabbage and pea soup greeted her, warmth of the stove battling the cold that stole in with her. They hugged then sat on the edge of her bed bowls in hand, Alicia's package between them. She opened it revealing ham and rye sandwiches, dunking them into the soup sucking out every last morsel of flavor until, reluctantly but satisfied, swallowing. She leant back against the wall drowsy, David's head on her shoulder.

"Gran?"

"Yes buddy."

"One day I'm going to have meat every week, and you will too."

"That's nice."

He sat up and, reaching in his pocket, put a torn page from a magazine in her hands.

"No, I mean it. I'm going to get this one day."

It was an augmentation service ad. All the trappings of success clearly and cleverly laid out around a young man who – as the ad boldly proclaimed – had been augmented. The price was breathtaking, easily more than she would earn in years. Too far out of reach to be practical, too close not to fuel frustration. She hugged David, handed it back to him.

"Always dream buddy, it's still the land of opportunity. One day, who knows?"

"It's no dream gran, it's going to happen. A warm house, nice food, new clothes, one day gran, one day." as he trailed off to sleep.

She rocked him gently as she silently wept.

The bus was colder now with winter coming on, shorter days with constant drizzle, no Victoria to keep her warm, fraying cardigan letting the wind from broken windows clutch at her. She could feel a cold coming on. For the first time in ages she felt old, could hear the years calling her.

She reached into her plastic bag for a tissue, coming up instead with a greasy shred of forgotten paper. She stared at the number, felt for the coin in her cardigan pocket. Hesitating only briefly she stood, alighted at the next stop and made the call.

It was like Victoria said, simple and easy. 'Of course she could.' they'd said and they'd come round, picked her up straight away. They'd even called the lady, made excuses for her, arranged a replacement. They were nice boys Alicia thought, nice boys.

They would pay her enough, oh yes more than enough and after she told them why they offered her more, if she could manage it. Of course, why not, the years of gravity fighting her body had to be of some use surely. And half now and half when back? No problem, none at all. They could even take her where she needed to go, take her home too if she liked. Very nice boys Alicia thought, considerate boys.

Alicia sat on the edge of the bed with David in the early morning. She felt younger, she'd had enough left over for a new blue ankle length dress, crocheted shawl, closed in shoes. It would not be right to travel in her work clothes. She kissed David on the head.

"It's only a week and a bit buddy, food is there and you'll be fine. They will come for you today, have you home by evening. It will all be fine."

David looked up, beaming.

"Thank you gran, I —"

"Shssh. Just make sure you relax, tell me all about it when I get back."

She moved to the door, looked back.

"All you have to worry about is what color the house will be."

She finished reading the formal statement and pressed her thumb to the corner of the page.

"It is all correct?"

"Yes."

The AI stood, retrieved the statement.

"The officer will take care of processing."

The eyes took a pair of handcuffs and approached her.

"Do I really need to use these? Will you give me any trouble?"

Alicia stood, straightened her dress and smiled.

"I will be fine, no trouble. You don't have to use them."

"Thank you."

Flanked by a medical orderly and her assistant they exited the room, walking down a windowless corridor towards glass doors.

The eyes saddened, it was like taking his mother to prison. An otherwise nice old lady, but for this one thing.

"First thing we need to do is get those extra organs out of you, fix the damage they may have done. They do lots of these, you'll be fine."

"Then?"

"Recovery, then sentencing. You've co-operated and been open, so that will help. The AIs take a dim view of anything else."

"Well, there's no point really, what's done is done."

They walked in silence, the only sounds shoes on tile, the air conditioners' hum.

"So how much did they promise you again?"

She told him.

It wasn't much. Two, perhaps three months wages for ten to twenty years in prison. He couldn't understand it, he never could reconcile risk to reward. They all knew they'd be caught eventually, the authorities or damage to their bodies catching up with them. He stopped, looked searchingly at her.

"Was it worth it?"

Alicia looked back steadily, without hesitation.

"Oh yes, definitely."

END

VOCATION

ABBOT JOHANNES GAZED at the twenty-four professed gathered before him, the bitter chill of early February penetrating the bare stone chapel. The taking of vows, the final irrevocable admission of a brother to the community was solemn, a time of thanks. This one was a unique, loss-tinged joy.

Having remained prostrated, naked in penitential reverence these past two days the supplicant at his feet lifted himself onto one knee, hands clasped in prayer, eyes locked on the Abbot's sandals.

Arms wide, head lifted to heaven, Abbot Johannes recited the ancient call to obedience and denial passed from Saint Benedict down the centuries, barely changed by the passage of time.

The supplicant stood, then raised his voice in reply.

"Iesus autem fidelis ad mortem, sicut et ego promitto stabilitatem meam, et oboedientiam usque ad mortem conversionem vitae."

One by one in absolute silence the professed greeted him with a brotherly kiss on the right cheek, then bade him farewell with a kiss on the left.

Once by themselves Abbot Johannes helped him onto the stretcher. He drank from a vial, lay flat and, with eyes shut and breath shallow, his body started to pale. Abbot Johannes hurriedly opened the chapel doors to four waiting, shivering figures. They ushered the stretcher to an ambulance, disappearing into the morning mist.

"God be with you Brother Angelo." Abbot Johannes whispered, closing the doors, shutting out the world.

Abbot Johannes regarded the Abbott General on his tablet. It was an unusual request, unprecedented for the *Ordo Cisterciensus Strictoris Observantiae*. A decision to be made, perhaps a life dedicated. Adjusting his glasses he referred to the sheaf of paper in his hands.

"It remains two hundred and fifty years?"

"At a minimum. Beyond that there are too many unknowns."

"They have no-one else?"

"Correct. If it were only a question of willingness there is no shortage. It is one of stability, obedience and reliability."

Abbot Johannes laid the papers carefully on his desk.

"Were their requirements a little broader I myself would consider it. The time is sufficient."

"Am I to understand the Abbey of Cuiaba has decided?"

"Yes, we accept with thanks."

"You have someone in mind, one who may be called?"

"One, a novice. This may be the hand of the divine."

"A novice? You are certain?"

"Yes. In three years he will be ready."

Monks' cells are by intent small, austere. Abbot Johannes sat on the plastic chair in one corner, knees touching the end of the bed. Novice Angelo sat at the head of the bed in the other corner.

"Brother Abbot, I am willing."

"You realize the uniqueness of the vocation? Your inclusion in and separation from the Order?"

"Yes."

"And the consequences?"

"That it is without repentance doubtless, yet so too my final vows."

Novice Angelo shifted slightly, long, slender fingers placing the papers back into their plastic folder.

"Did not our Lord challenge us to cut off the limb that causes us to sin? It is a blessing, a humbling gift. Prayer and contemplation, my work to support the Order, what more could there be to my life?"

Abbot Johannes stood.

"Your novitiate will be like no other. There are preparations to be made, designs to be finished. Apart from the Congregation of Divine Worship and the Discipline of the Sacraments you will live as a hermit, see only those who must see you, speak only with me. A test of your vocation, trial before commitment."

They knew him as no other man had been known. When they bid him come he bore the probing and sampling and scanning silently, obediently, gracefully. When the men and women with pocket protectors and iPads and security passes left he thanked God for the sweats, chills, the burning daggers and aches in his body, the chance to turn it to dust. Repeated through the days and weeks to months and years in his cell that was his world, vigils through compline sung by one to the Almighty, the Almighty to one, his vocation strengthened, so too the faith of Abbot Johannes in him.

They bought it to him the week before his vows. It was not as he had imagined, rather a vessel of simple beauty in keeping with the Order. No signs of science or technology but a pewter gray unadorned chalice. They alone would bear him away, move him forward and care until it was no longer possible they said; for they had grown to love and cherish him. He allowed himself the luxury of words, his first to them, thanking God for the work of their hands. With the ancient rites he blessed them, their children, families, health and lives until in tears and peace they left him alone to prepare.

Brother Angelo returned one week later to be interred. They lowered him into the earth, not with traditional words and incantations but with ones written by the Abbot, ones befitting the commitment of a temple lacking the holy of holies.

Abbot Johannes imagined Brother Angelo rising from the earth on a tail of fire. They could not sustain the body for that time and distance, but the mind was another thing. He smiled. A Trappist monk sent to Eris was poetic, fitting. Named after the Greek goddess of discord and strife Eris would receive an envoy of the Prince of Peace.

What would he find beyond Pluto, the feeble Sun's rays six hours away, a year stretched five hundred and fifty fold? Brother Angelo's thirty-year journey will see me in my grave yet they say he will have five hundred years now, perhaps a thousand. While unseen and unheard his subconscious automatically controls the systems, feeds and telemetry to and from the radio telescope, his conscious mind will be unburdened, free to the discipline of meditation, quietude and receptivity.

Absolute solitude.

Unassailed silence.

Total separation from the world.

Abbot Johannes felt the first pangs of envy. He turned from the graveside.

END

LOVE IS THE DRUG

FURNITURE OF MEMORY latex and plasteel, ceramics decorating walls and floors, windows of smart glass. A clean, harsh, efficiently depressing air bringing the silence of the tomb to the hospital.

Emily and Tasha were with the specialist. The door opened and Dr. Heres motioned James inside, pointing to a solitary chair on the far side of the room. James seated himself quietly.

Tasha glowered at him, a seven year old well versed in the social mores and norms placing her above all men, her father included. Father. A word out of time, an anachronistic biological label. None of his genes resided in Tasha, nothing of who he was. A man was simply of use, every woman requiring an other for certain necessary tasks. They knew best, said it made for a better society. Twenty-eight years of conditioning told him so; centuries of history simply reinforced the belief. It was as it was, as it should be, and he was Emily's.

Dr. Heres drummed her fingers on the desk. James had let his mind wander again. He settled, hands in lap, silent.

"I will make this as simple as possible for you James. If Emily wishes you to know more it is up to her."

"Thank you."

"Tasha has a very serious illness. It will be extremely difficult to treat. For the next five months you must be extra careful and attentive and make no mistakes. Most importantly do not upset or anger her. Is that clear?"

"Yes. No mistakes, no anger, no upset."

Dr. Heres turned to Emily.

"I will leave any further discussion to you. Obviously mortality projections are beyond him."

"It's best not to confuse him. This much is enough."

He sat quietly. He'd told no-one he had learned to read and write. Illegal, it was forbidden by law and church as folly taunting men into believing they could leave their preordained place. He did not know what mortality meant, but he knew mortal was about life so maybe Tasha was in deep trouble.

Dr. Heres ushered Emily and Tasha out, ignoring James' thin, quiet frame nestled in the corner. She was just about to shut the door behind her when she noticed him.

"Shouldn't you be taking them home?"

"She's dying isn't she?"

"I've told you all Emily wants you to know."

James stood, hesitated.

"Please, you know they will tell me no more."

"It's for your own good. You have a home to run. It's too much to worry your pretty head about."

"At least let me have a name for what she has."

She looked at him, her scowl softening to pity. Stupid men never know when to stop, when it's better not to know.

"Fine. It's called Kavoort's Syndrome. Now go."

They were waiting under the awning looking at the car through the rain. Emily barely glanced at him, Tasha with folded arms contemptuously ignoring him. He took the umbrella and escorted them across the three meter gap being careful to keep them perfectly dry. Once they were seated, car door closed, he folded the umbrella and went to the open driver's compartment, the wind-blown rain falling harder, scouring his face.

She'd required him that evening. His energy had risen to meet her need, now she lay propped up against the pillows watching him dress. He stood, back towards her in mock bashfulness, careful to make sure the mirrors reflected him back to her as he knew she liked.

Tasha lay absentmindedly on her bed in the attached room. She was disinterested now, but the time would come when Emily would introduce her to this pleasure through him, with him. She would learn her skills at his hands before selecting her own. If she lived.

The tiniest flicker of sorrow showed before he recomposed himself, pulled the veneer of thankful ecstasy back. It was not unnoticed, Emily pointing to the bed beside her, motioning him to sit.

She ran her fingers through his dreadlocks.

"This is why we don't tell you everything, it only worries you. It's nothing you can understand. There's more tests, more examinations. If you want to help just keep doing your best around the house."

James nodded.

"Now off you go."

James stood, made his way back to his quarters.

Leon closed the washer and hit the deep cycle button.

"Well of course she's right, just settle down and keep house."

He sat next to James, the plastic chair gently protesting.

"Why on earth you'd want to interfere in women's business I have no idea. Here I was thinking you were a fine upstanding boy and you're wanting to disturb the natural order of things?"

James bristled slightly.

"It's not that, I just want to help. I feel so useless, what good's a clean house and fresh clothes if she's so sick?"

Leon jabbed his finger at him, cigarette ash landing on James' knee.

"It's the foundation of the family, stability to weather the storms of life."

He quoted directly from Sunday school.

"Adam came first imperfect and flawed, then Eve next to be obeyed and adored. Our job is to support and help, not interfere."

"I suppose so."

"No suppose at all." adjusting his codpiece, trying to avoid the chafe. "Let them take care of the big stuff."

Katie waved at James from behind the counter, motioning him over. She owned the laundromat and was on society's fringe, a threat to the girls, friend to the boys.

"So what's up Jim, trouble in paradise?"

He told her, although it hurt his head just remembering the details.

"Well they'd say that wouldn't they. Do you want me to find out for you?"

She pulled out her interface.

"It's not good. Tasha's dying Jim."

Although he suspected, hearing it spoken was like calling it into existence. The cold gnawing at him wasn't from the air-conditioner.

"So what's the cure?"

She leant forwards, tapping and scrolling for a few minutes.

"It's weird, they don't say."

It was more than James' inbred politeness could take.

"What's wrong, what do you see?"

Katie looked up, made sure they were alone.

"Only if you can keep it a secret. And I'm serious, not even to Leon."

"Yes, yes, whatever you want."

"There's no cure here. But it seems like there is one off-world, and if I read it right it's just one injection and it's done."

"So I could just buy it?"

"No, it's banned. They'll never let it in."

"Why?"

"Hon, it's based on boy hormones. Only girls get the disease, it's rare and always fatal. But if boy hormones cure it then that makes girls dependent on boys and that is not allowed, you know that."

"That's not fair, I'll do it anyway, I'll get some and bring it to her."

"Nobody travels off-world; nobody comes, nobody goes. It's only the automatic cargo ships that visit and they're guarded."

She looked at his face, surprised it was streaked with tears.

"You love Tasha don't you?"

James nodded.

"If there was a way —"

"In a second, of course I would."

"I thought so. If it was very risky, very expensive?"

"No difference."

"Maybe, just maybe I can help. Sit here and wait, don't go

anywhere."

She stood up, moved to a small curtained doorway.

"I'll be a few minutes, I need to talk to someone. Take care of the store and don't leave."

When Katie stepped back into the empty laundromat it was a huge relief for James, having spent the last few hours alternating between fear of the responsibility thrust upon him and pleasure seeing the other boys' faces as they came in. She walked past him and threw the bolt on the door.

"If you're still serious there's a way, but it's going to cost you three days, seven hundred creds. Can you get the time and money?"

Time was no problem, he had just over a year's vacation in hand. The money was a third of his life savings but that didn't matter. He offered Katie his forearm.

"Yes, yes I can, right now if you like."

She pushed it back.

"Not so quick, hear me out first. My friend can get you out and back as live cargo, sealed in a coffin carrier. When they unload someone will give you the treatment, send you home the same way. We unpack you three days later when you get back. But you have to go tomorrow."

"Fine. But how do I go to the toilet or eat? Three days is a long time."

"Not for you it won't be. It will be three days here but to you it will be three to four hours. It's all FTL, all you do is go before they seal you in."

"I don't understand."

"You don't have to hon, don't worry your pretty self over it. Just trust me. Now are you in?"

"Of course."

Katie took his arm, swiped his wrist over the terminal. Once it had flashed confirmation she let go.

"Come back here first thing tomorrow morning, bring a blanket and no food or drink from now on."

James hit his head on the seat bulkhead as the ground car came to a halt. Feet moved outside, the trunk opening to blinding light, hands hurrying him out.

"No time to waste, let's go."

He stood inside a large, cluttered storage shed. Katie stood with two other women in front of a black, rectangular box. She pointed to it.

"That's it, lie as flat as you can, get as comfy as you can. Denise managed to get you a padded one."

He tucked the blanket in tightly around him, tapped the stopwatch function on his bracelet.

"Thank you Katie."

They brought the lid over, hooked it to the end of the box.

"Now remember. You'll go from here to the cargo ship, get loaded on and go. About an hour later you'll be offloaded and someone will hand you the treatment. Don't do anything, don't get out of the coffin, keep quiet. They'll load you back on and in three hours we'll unpack you. Any questions?"

"No."

"Happy travels Jim."

They lowered the lid, sealing out the light and noise, sealing him in with the faint glow of his wristband.

It was smooth, silent, cold. He'd toyed with not bringing the blanket but was now glad he had one that could be tucked right around him, behind and in front.

His wristband barely flashed 01:29 when the lid opened a crack, admitting a pale shaft of yellow light. A hand thrust itself in, clutching a small flask. James stared at hairy, stubby fingers ending in cracked and dirty nails, the middle finger beyond the second knuckle missing. It was a boy's hand, an ancient boy's hand.

It wiggled, agitated. James reached up, tugged the flask easily away and placed it snugly by his side. The hand slid out, the lid dropping and sealing with a hiss.

"Harriss, you got another one there?"

Tony looked up, his supervisor favoring him with a bored and listless gaze.

"You know how it is Ted, a bit extra for the kids and missus."

"Yeah, and now your boss. What this time?"

"Broad spectrum hormones, single shot." He jabbed a thumb at the coffin. "Got one shipped himself in and out as cargo just to pick it up."

"Morons. You'd think they'd lift the embargo, make it easier. Anyway he's got more trouble now. They've reassigned the FTL, all this is going back standard lightspeed."

"You're kidding, sixty years objective?"

"I know, I know, that's the government for you, just flick of a switch. Anyway, can't keep him here, no visa."

"I guess."

"You got paid didn't you?"

"Up front, of course."

"No issue then. You're paid, he's got what he wanted and he won't know until he gets back home."

"Still seems rough, maybe I should tell him?"

"Nah, wouldn't bother. He'll only get upset, you know how they bring them up. Anyway, any chance to stick it that damned bunch of amazons is a good thing."

Tony smiled, hit the customs seal.

"Yeah, you're right. I'll load them up straight away."

James was worried. His wristband showed 05:46, he was uncomfortable, there was no sign of Katie, and no one had opened his lid. How long until my air runs out, or I get another serious cramp, or heaven forbid my bowels can't hang on any longer?

The lid came off without warning, one instant pitch black the next blinding white light. James lay frozen, blinking as his eyes adjusted. A face framed by red hair, raised eyebrows and a yellow vest gazed down at him.

"Now just what have we got here?"

She pointed to a bench leaning against the nearest wall.

"Get out boy, go sit."

James hopped out, sat down. He started to knead his protesting calves, pushing away the pins and needles. The woman just stared at him.

"Long trip I'd guess. You hungry, thirsty?"

"No ma'am, no thank you."

"Well at least your manners are good. What's your name boy?"

He looked around, his eyes now used to the light. He was sure it was the same storage shed, the logos and roof were identical but it seemed dirtier, ragged around the edges. Faint daylight of an early morning sun cascaded through open doors. He couldn't see Katie anywhere.

"I said, what's your name boy?"

"Sorry ma'am, it's James."

She scowled at him, took a step backwards.

"Well James, you have some explaining to do. Stay right here until I get back."

She walked to a small staircase. Once she came back, once they found out where he'd been these past three days he was sure he was in serious trouble. More importantly Tasha would not get the cure, Katie was clear about that, they wouldn't let her have it.

She stopped at the top of the stairs, turning to give him one more scowl. She opened a door and stepped inside, disappearing from sight.

James grabbed the flask from the coffin and ran through the open doors, down the pathway and along the street. It was cold, the street slippery under his bare feet, but he hardly noticed. He ran past a parked taxi, stopped, went back and jumped in.

"Presier 26C, North View please."

The driver pointed to a screen on the seat back. James placed his arm on it, the fare jumped across, and the taxi pulled out into light traffic. The screen briefly flashed up his savings balance, sixty-two thousand one hundred creds. He shook his head as the numbers faded, it was clearly wrong, way too much but there were bigger things to worry about.

The driver stared at him in the rear view mirror.

"Aren't you a bit chilly hun?"

"Well, yes ma'am, a bit I guess."

"I mean I like the old fashioned gear but it's winter you know, you gotta take care of your assets."

"I know it's last year's but I dressed in a hurry this morning."

"More like last century, but each to his own, each to his woman's needs."

The taxi came to a halt.

"This be your stop. Have peace."

James hopped out, watched the taxi move off. Snowflakes landed on his nose and hair, soft wet splotches. The wheels in his mind started to grind. Winter? It was summer when I left, hot, sticky, raining. Katie got it wrong, I've been gone months! Tasha? Is she still alive, am I too late? He clutched the flask tighter, turned to face the house.

He was sure it was the right place, but the garden was gone, replaced with sculpted concrete, a low stone wall and water features. The house was the wrong color, the curtains plain not floral, roof aerials replaced by a single silver-gray dish. The cold reached into his bones. So much change, so quickly? His feet carried him to the door, his hand reaching for the doorknob, cold brass pressing chilled flesh. He hesitated, pulled his hand away and reached instead for the doorbell.

A boy his age in a satin sash and toga answered the door.

"Now just how do I go about helping you bro?"

The words stuck, jumbled as they fell from his mouth.

"Tasha, Emily, I, I'm, James, home."

"I see. No, I really don't. Wait here."

The boy closed the door on him.

I'm gone three days, three days or even a few months and Emily's replaced me with that?

The door opened. A vaguely familiar face stared at him with contempt. It was lined, aged, thinning gray hair, her stooped frame leaning on a walking stick.

"Well well, you finally come skulking back do you now?"

"I'm sorry Emily, it took longer than they said, they lied to me."

He held the flask out to her with both hands.

"But I got it, I got the treatment for Tasha, she can be cured, get rid of the disease."

She glowered at him, then lashed out with the walking stick sending the flask crashing into ground. The vial inside bounced free, hit the concrete and shattered. James watched on in horror as the orange-yellow liquid drained away.

The walking stick swung back, catching James across his knees, sending him down in front of her. The point caught him under the chin, lifting his face up to look at her.

"Idiot! She's been dead these past twenty years and you know what, all she worried about was where you had run off to. The diagnosis was wrong, didn't we tell you not to worry?"

"She's dead? Tasha's dead?"

The woman laughed, a coarse hacking noise.

"You always were stupid James. I'm Tasha, it's Emily that's dead!"

"Tasha? No, you can't —"

"Yes, it's me. Sixty-one years you've been gone. No-one waits that long."

Tasha turned to the boy, slowly walked back into the house.

"Reggie, please dispose of the old furniture."

END

BACON BUTTER

I GOT THIS thing for butter. Not the mass-produced stuff but boutique, Sorrell melt in your mouth handmade creamy delight. It's expensive but I budget to the cent, autopay all my bills. All I see is my drinking and grocery money.

Well, truth is the one hundred forty-nine dollars and ninety-nine cents drinking money's exactly Uncle Owen's fine for public disturbance. He's a fair and reasonable public official even if he is on the bench. Got to the point last year I sent the fines straight through in advance. I'm a little calmer now, not much sense in using all my drinking money to fight.

But no matter what I always have my eight dollars ninety-five for my butter. So last thing Thursdays, car full of groceries and eight ninety-five in my pocket I stop by Eli's Deli and pick it up. This time it's the last one on the shelf.

"Hey Eli! You got anything fresher?"

He waddles out the back, he likes his butter too. At least bricklaying burns it off me.

"Hell no, can't you read?" pointing to the sign, knowing full well I can't. "It's the last, Sorrell's gone belly up."

I'm gutted. I'm not the only one, the short guy near the door's heartbroken. It's great butter, try it half an inch thick on your brioche and tell me the heart attack's not worth it.

I got mine so I toss my money at Eli and head out the door.

"Hey mister, how much you want for the butter?"

I turn around. There's shorty.

"It's not for sale, go get your own."

"I'll give you twenty dollars."

"No dice."

"Fifty?"

"Nope, not for sale."

"How 'bout one forty-nine ninety-nine? Hear you could use it."

I give him the evil eye.

"I told you it's not for sale. Why you so interested?"

"I promised a friend I'd bring her back some. Let me buy you a drink, I got something to trade, something you might like. If you're not interested after that, fair enough."

What the hell, a free drink's a no-brainer. We walk half a block and settle into a corner at the Biker Bar. It's familiar, I know the barmaids and a fair few feet of the floor intimately.

He shows me his wristband.

"How'd you like Uncle Owen to never see your ugly face again? This'll let you start, make and get out of trouble scot-free. Now pick someone, anyone."

Propping up the bar in front of us is Big Dave. We go back a long way, I lost my virginity to his girlfriend and he gave me my first broken nose. Over the years his waistline grew to match his six four height. Better than most I knew that ninety-five percent of that wasn't fat. I lean across to shorty.

"How about the guy in the Comanchero colors?"

"No problem. First, I press the red part of the wristband."

He wanders over, elbows in between Dave and some other guy wearing colors. Dave turns, slowly, looking down.

"Excuse me?"

"Oh I'm sorry petal. Let me buy you a drink."

Turning to the barmaid he yells "Two strawberry daiquiris sweetie!"

The crowded bar goes silent. The barmaid's blowing the dust off an old cocktail leaflet and Dave's glowing red under his bandanna.

Shorty turns to the other guy.

"I apologize if I've upset your girlfriend, is it her time of month?" Then, turning to Dave, "It's ok, I understand how delicate and fragile you must be feeling."

Dave's neck disappears into his shoulders as he gives me a

withering gaze. I shake my head and hold up my hands. I'm here to watch the show not star in it.

"Anyway," shorty continues, one hand on Dave's leg and one finger to his lips "didn't I see you at Mardi Gras ... oh no, that's it, you were handing out how to vote cards for Hillary weren't you?"

Dave grabs shorty by the neck, lifting him off the floor. I go straight for my phone's paramedic speed dial.

"Oh we are trifle prickly aren't we?" and in a blink shorty's got Dave's hand off, thumb broken and head smashed into the bar. Dave crumples to the floor. Shorty dispatches the other guy with a rapid left-right combo.

No one moves. The barmaid places two perfect strawberry daiquiris down. Shorty picks them up, sets them on our table.

Shorty presses the blue section of his wristband.

"Now part two."

Everyone looks around as if it's all news to them. 'What the hell?' and 'How'd this happen?' is all I hear, nobody's got a clue not even Dave who's lifting himself by a barstool off the floor.

Shorty leans back, smirking.

"Now you tell me that's not worth the butter."

I had it out in a jiffy.

"Sounds fair to me."

He takes the butter and holds out the wristband.

"Just one thing," keeping hold, pressing a yellow section "you can dump it all on someone else if they're dumb enough." with which shorty, butter and wristband wink out of existence.

"Well aint you the gutsy one?" I hear as I turn around, the bar closing in.

There went another one forty-nine ninety-nine and a week in hospital.

Another Thursday, another trip to Eli's. I've gone right off butter but bacon's another thing.

The space for the highland Fitzroy bacon's nearly empty.

"Oh come on Eli, you gotta have more than that!"

"The hell I do! Fitzroy's folded, that's it."

I buy it all, maybe I'll grow my own pigs.

"Excuse me sonny, how much do you want for the bacon?"

I turn around to see a little old lady looking up at me from under her Sunday best bonnet.

A right uppercut lays her out cold in the pickle and sausage aisle.

Damn aliens. I know just where that was headed and I don't get paid till Thursday week.

END

GLASS HALF OVERFULL

It was a warm, bright morning, Yannis' clicking hooves and swaying cart conspiring against Orestes to call him back to sleep he had barely risen from. It was harder getting up these days, never mind doing what needed to be done, winter mornings enticing him to lie in nestled against the mild chill, summer mornings cocooning him with the promise of warm, idle, lazy days. Thankfully Yannis had no such issues.

They plodded slowly out of Limoni. Behind them the Aegean's blue sky stained dirty brown, before them Olympus, the abode of the gods abandoning man to his fate, this man to his. A tiny shower of stones came from the left, half hearted listless projectiles falling short of Yannis who ignored them, the clip of his hooves keeping their rhythm.

"Oi, Orest, does it smell having your head up your ass old man?" the boys called, lying back against the low stone wall, beer and cigarettes between them. One pulled another handful of gravel, considered tossing it then gave up in favor of another drink, making do with a sullen, bored glance.

Orestes ignored them as he did each morning, not out of hatred but rather habit. Drinking at this hour was not acceptable, but what else is there for them? No work, small town and little to distract they had nothing to think of but the next support payment, beer and sleep. The wonder of it was they weren't up to worse than annoying an old man.

He pulled Yannis to the right, heading to the Litocharo estate and the new excavations. A few kilometers and a few more minutes to think, to let the sun warm his bones. It was good enough to keep him occupied and fed, a few euros letting him scrabble around the rubble before the Antiquities people arrived. Thank the gods for cashed up and ignorant American tourists willing to pay for shards of pottery or tiles but more importantly the tale, a pitch of antiquity and permanence they somehow could not find at home.

The site was deserted, the gate unchained as he passed through. He tied Yannis to a nearby shrub then carefully clambered down, one hand against the earth wall, an empty basket in the other, cheroot between teeth. Already the lines for the footings were faintly marked. It had been a good site so far, hopefully this last day would see more.

It was tiring but fruitful work, Orestes stretching the kinks from his back a few hours later, basket half full of broken pottery, blue and black tiles. Some were in remarkable condition, barely scratched but clearly old, perfect specimens for a museum or local history association, but they didn't pay and a man can't live on air.

The ground was now completely picked over, sun high and hot, time to go and rest to prepare for tonight's bartering among the hotels and restaurants along the coast. Basket in hand Orestes turned to leave when a glint caught his eye. Moving closer he could see a small lip of black and gold glazing poking out of the wall, barely above the floor. He took his penknife from his pocket and started to scrape away the dirt.

It took only a short time to free the object, now revealed as a small porcelain jar. He could not see the outside for hardened dirt, but knew it would be worth a tidy sum once cleaned up. Orestes removed his shirt, wrapped the jar inside it, and placed it on top of the basket.

Yannis clopped steadily past the boys, now lying sleeping in the sun, their drunken stupor bringing renewed promises of sunburn and hangovers. He ignored the snoring Orestes behind him, ignored the flowers and sweet grass growing in the school yard and made his way steadily through Limoni to the decrepit brown house and yard that was their home. He nosed through the open gate to the olive tree, stopping in the shade. He was old, the man was old, and if the man could drift off again well so could he. It wasn't long until

Orestes' and Yannis' snores cycled together, a synchronized rasp-hasp floating through the air.

What is this place? Ornate, large, but whose? Orestes couldn't even imagine this much marble, the gold and silver inlay, billowing silk curtains and luxurious – if a little old fashioned – furniture. Clearly I'm in trouble, this is either the judge's or magistrate's home but I can't recall what it was I did. Crystal placed on stone turned Orestes around. A fresh faced, confident young man reclined on a marble daybed, offhandedly examining him.

"Welcome Orestes. Please, have a seat."

He tried to place the face. It was familiar in a way, but stubbornly refused to be identified.

"I don't believe I know you."

"Oh no, you don't and I don't expect you will. Excuse my manners, it's been a while since I've had … company. My name is Epimethus. You've heard of me?"

"The Epimethus? Prometheus' —"

"The one and the same, although I'm starting to despair that anyone remembers."

"So I must be dead?"

"Oh no, nothing like that. You're just enjoying a little nap at home and I thought I'd drop in, you know, have a chat while your mind was open. Remarkable little donkey you have too, wonderful little beast, I must get one."

Epimethus sat up, leant forward eagerly.

"When I said 'a chat' I really do have something I need you to do for me. Your little expedition this morning, you found a small jar, about so high?" He held his hands slightly apart. "A black and gold affair, thick necked?"

"I found something like it, I've yet to clean it up."

"Yes, yes, that's it, that's the one."

"You want to buy it? You have cash?"

"Oh no, no, I simply want you to put it back in the ground, bury it nice and deep for me. Perhaps under all that concrete your nephew will pour tomorrow."

"Why would I do that? It'll fetch me a good price."

"Is that better than getting on my good side?"

Why can't I have those simple, uncomplicated dreams I used to have? Why always trouble, problems?

"All I want is a quiet life, a little money, a little drink now and then. The jar's mine to sell or keep, why should I bury it?"

"You see, it used to belong to my wife, well she had a little trouble with it a while ago, you know, pestilence, sorrow, pain and such so we had it buried. Didn't think anyone would find it, obviously you did, we didn't have concrete in those days, wonderful stuff, it would've done the job nicely. Father is still pretty upset over the whole thing so, if you could, it would help."

"Well, I'll have to think about it, especially if it's valuable."

"It's just trouble, it needs to be buried. We've still got a little pull down there so if it's favors you need —"

"It gets harder each year, my knees aren't what they used to be but if you could see your way, you know, with the tiles and tourists?"

"I can see what I can do but I'm afraid our time's up."

"Oh?"

"Yes, I think your neighbor's trying to wake you."

Yannis watched Ilias trying to get Orestes' attention, first by whispers then by a gentle rocking. The young man simply didn't understand the old man's capacity or need for sleep, and if he chose to sleep the afternoon away who's to judge him for that? Unfortunately it was also Yannis' time to rest, to relax until tomorrow when he would slowly haul his cargo and master round the streets, and the young man was disturbing him. Enough was enough. He shook his head, let out a loud bray, then took two rapid steps forwards then two more backwards.

Orestes woke immediately, sat up to see Ilias regarding him with a wry smile. He retrieved the crushed cheroot, placing it between his teeth, then swung down from the cart.

"I was wondering where you were, been waiting ages for you."

He held out the basket, tucked the jar under his arm.

"Lend a hand could you and carry this for me? We can talk over some tea."

It was sweet and hot, refreshing outside in the afternoon breeze.

Ilias sat legs thrust forwards, staring into space. Orestes leant back having placed the jar carefully in a bucket of water. An hour or so, maybe less, the dirt should fall away and I'll have it clean, maybe even unscratched. He relit his cheroot, sent a ring of dense gray smoke spinning upwards.

"So, what news?"

"Nothing good as always. It spreads a little slower, a little quieter, but it is still there, still eating her away."

"How is she today?"

"Today is good, she has the fight back, her toughness. More tests, stronger treatments they say and she pins her heart on them."

Ilias shrugged, resignedly.

"A little more money, a few years earlier, even a bigger country or different treatments, but as it is …"

Orestes grabbed the younger man's shoulder, gave him a solid, fatherly shake.

"She needs your strength, calmness, even when there is none she needs to see hope fight in you."

Five years I watched Damara struggle, fight back and try, five years of playing the rock for her to lean on, to stand with. No time for tears and doubt then, time enough the twenty years after.

"You know I'm right Ilias, you know that."

"Of course I know. At times I feel like giving in, but fight on we will, I will."

"Good. And I am here for you both."

He reached under the table, bought out a half-full bottle and two small glasses. He filled them quickly.

"Health and success. May you both live long enough to embarrass your great-grandchildren."

Maybe it had been a mistake bringing the bottle out but sometimes it was needed. With Ilias gone and the bottle nearly empty Orestes knew he would not be selling anything that evening. There would be other tourists tomorrow night and a chance to atone for his laziness. A bottle deserved to be either full or empty, not stuck in some strange middle state. He refilled his glass, looked to the bucket of muddied water at his feet.

It was lovely, black gold and, more importantly as he pulled it out and slowly turned it around, the enamel was blemish free and the stopper still in. I will have to find a special friend for this piece, an old sentimental friend with a fat wallet indeed. Perhaps I will even have some spare for poor Ilias' wife. He placed the jar carefully down out of the way, drained his glass in one swallow. The gentle evening breeze carrying tantalizing hints of dinner and dessert from the neighbors lulled him asleep.

"So, have you thought it over?"

Epimethus sat opposite him astride Yannis. How he'd managed to get the donkey into the marble house was beyond him but if it is a dream why not? If it's my dream why am I not in control?

"In fact, I might even add a little bit in for Yannis here, I think we have a deep connection."

"It's still no to both. He may not be much but he's my only transport, and that jar's going to make me a nice little sum."

Epimethus now sat next to him, Yannis nowhere to be seen.

"You really haven't been listening. Orestes, the jar isn't empty. Do you remember who the jar belonged to?"

"You said it was your wife."

"And she is?"

"Mrs. Epimethus?"

He gave an exasperated sigh, closed his eyes then took a deep breath.

"Look, I'll make it easy for you. Seven letters, starts with 'P' and ends in 'andora'. So?"

"Pandora?"

"Thank you, finally! Your kind can be so frustrating. So it's her jar, the one with the evils, we put the lid back on but there's something left, something I want to keep in."

Orestes could vaguely remember the myths he was told as a child, Pandora's jar, how she'd left something in and now Epimethus wanted him to bury it? Now what was it again?

"Hope."

"What?"

"Hope, there's hope in the jar and you want me to leave it there."

"Well yes, of course, why else would I bother getting in touch?"

"I could have done with more hope when Damara died and Ilias needs as much as he can get now. Why would I leave it bottled up?"

"It's not good for you and once out you can't put it back! Don't you think we tried with death? Well, you know how well that worked."

"How can you say hope's bad?"

"It's not been stored in a jar of goodies has it? No, it was in a jar of evils, you work it out."

"But we've already got hope, how can more be anything but good?"

"Your hope is tainted, tainted by fear and imagination and desire, it keeps you striving, bettering, trying to do whatever it is you do even if you know it's futile. But this hope's pure, empty, it's — You know, you really ought to cut back on the ouzo Orestes."

"What?"

"Your bladder's too old, you're waking up again and don't open the jar!"

The pain was intense, remnant kidney stones screaming at him as he relieved himself against the olive tree. Should know better at my age, she'd shout at me if she knew I was drinking again, if she caught me peeing outdoors. Gods how I miss her shouting.

Cotton-mouthed and dopey Orestes made his way back to the jar, picking it up to take it inside safe for the night. It was beautiful even with the slight sludge along one side. He leant forward to pick up his shirt, to polish the jar clean, and even as he did so felt the jar slip slowly, gently but determinedly out of his grasp. He turned his head just in time to see the jar bounce once then shatter into a hundred pieces. The gentle evening breeze paused, changed direction, carrying faint women's laughter as it shifted again.

It was a shame, but one jar meant one customer, a hundred pieces a hundred customers. Orestes stepped over the shards into the house. They were there now, they would be there when he needed them. Tomorrow, the next day, whenever. There would always be shards, always be tourists, always be time.

It was good to be free of the harness, not to drag the old man and the cart around. He was sitting on the chair near the back door, cup of tea in hand smiling and waving at him as he meandered out the gate.

"Enjoy yourself, come back when you want, why waste a beautiful day?"

Yannis was a little confused, but not enough to stop and go back. Why the old man didn't want to work was none of his business. He passed the young man sitting with his wife outside their door, sharing their morning coffee.

The woman turned to the man, beaming.

"I don't think I'll go anymore Ilias, I feel so much better, so healthy and fit, it's already beaten, I know it is."

The young man leant across, hugged her tightly.

"Yes, I'm sure of it. There's no point wasting our time or such a good day when everything will work out anyway."

Yannis turned the corner, headed away from Limoni towards Olympus. The young boys sat in the morning sun, sharing a cigarette and bottle. Instead of stones they threw waves at him, smiling, laughing.

"Burro, hey burro, wonderful morning burro!"

Their voices receded as Yannis clopped away, calling greetings to each passer by.

"Now that's much better isn't it?"

Yannis didn't break stride, simply turned his head to the fresh faced, confident young man sitting astride him. He seemed to weigh nothing and lacked the old man's muddy, stale breakfast smell.

Epimethus lay down along Yannis' back, his head lying cheek down between the donkey's ears.

"Oh indeed you are a remarkable little donkey, a wonderful little beast! Just wait until they see you at home. And to think you only cost me one old jar."

END

LAZARUS

IT'S NOWHERE NEAR dawn, my eyes open, I tense. Dark is never dark, she lies, watches, smiles. Her hand reaches out, caresses my face.

'Just checking.' she whispers.

'You expected?'

'This, you, alive, my miracle.'

Miracle. The children follow me as I go, parents watch from doorways, pull their families away half scared, half envious, all covetous. I never asked for it, never sought him out or made promises, yet here am I, a ghost made flesh, the once dead once more among the living. The resurrection. The miracle. A stranger in the village I was born, raised, died.

'Rise once, then rise again.'

The stone bounces off my shoulder, skips ahead into the fields. I turn, Ruth pulls back, curses me from under her shawl, tears for her husband lost, venom for the one brought back instead of her beloved. My hand comes away bloodied, memories of worse and deeper as blades slashed, cut deep, unbidden reminders I am no more of them, of my line. Another small scar, my body through life unblemished save calloused hands until, afterwards, they test me, prod me, hate, wish. I lift my feet deliberately, rapidly, the dust of the village falls away as I continue alone.

The rabbi moves off the path, his disciples hurry heads down

115

after him, sway as they give me wide berth, deny my existence. As much as they wanted him dead they want me, yet fear of what may happen stays their hand. Rumours persist of an empty tomb, apparitions, visitations; yet for each a hundred others of stolen corpses, far travels, the work of demons and devils on weak minds and weaker hearts. For me it matters not; the faith of my fathers is denied me by those who guard it, and he fails to return.

The sun is low, the afternoon cool when hobbling, bent-limbed, the branch seconded for his deformed leg digging deep he climbs, wearied but determined, to me.

'If I can but touch you I will be restored.'

I touch him. I touch him again, and again. Each my fist, my feet, my staff harder, merciless to his joints, his infirmities, his screams and piteous cries as he tumbles down, crawls away as broken in spirit as in body.

'Idiot! You want what is not mine to give? Better to walk through life crippled then through death's door once.'

Yet twice will I walk through it. Righteous in death I stood with Abraham four days then, dragged back to the living, cursed by the sorcery of my sisters' and wife's tears upon him, I am reborn. To what? Uncertainty, unable to sacrifice, pray, show obedience, I am left without place, without hope, without understanding. Even yet my body curses me, screams for rest, its time yet done, but I am poured in anew. I do not fit, it does not belong, yet are we here.

To the west lies what I knew, the land of my fathers, my family, my life, my death, the memory of the one who who returned me unbidden for his glory, his cause, his followers' faith.

To the east the desert, the wandering years of Moses and Joshua, the land of my people saved yet lost, purposeless, confused.

I turn my back to the setting sun and walk.

END

SLIVER

It was a good landing, smooth and boring. Gordon released the hatch and stepped out getting his first real view of the surface. Just as advertised, featureless and barren, an unbroken series of low mounds and shallow valleys carved in yellow-brown sand and rock. No buildings, no sign of any human habitation save the fused circle his slipship sat on and the ribbon of hard packed yellow leading away to a solitary autodrive. Reclusive hermits, clearly the Brotherhood took their vows and their planet seriously. He took his grip, sealed the hatch.

The autodrive activated as he neared.

"Gordon Suzman?"

"Yes."

The autodrive's roof and sides dissolved revealing an austere, serviceable cabin. He put his grip in the back, following it onto the curved bench.

The roof and sides reformed.

"Opaque or clear?"

"Clear."

The autodrive accelerated between the hummocks, a russet prune sliding along a custard landscape. Gordon leant back, looked around the cabin in vain for any AV devices. Nothing, not even ancient audio. He settled a little further into the bench, as far as the thin padding would allow. It would be different not being plugged in and networked all the time, unpleasant perhaps but an experience anyway. Three days would be more than enough of this place for him and he was sure it would be enough for them. They were not unwelcoming, simply cautious, and had made him agree to a short but very specific set of guidelines before coming, mainly restrictions on movement and communication. Which suited him fine, he wasn't coming to see anyone anyway, it was too late for that.

"In bound, audio only, Prelate." the autodrive announced.

He closed his eyes to concentrate, remember the briefing notes. Each member of the Brotherhood had a closely monitored and rigidly enforced annual permissible quota of spoken words. Their speech had changed over the centuries to a highly compressed pidgin, a reduced vocabulary based on the most common interactions. It was not the understanding that would test him, rather making responses in kind that would not require response in turn. Out of duty the Prelate would respond to an outsider, even to exceeding the quota and incurring sanction. He would use a week's worth on Gordon, and Gordon had no desire to exceed it.

"Eternal. Safe, comfortable, needful?"

"Eternal indeed." Gordon responded after the ancient manner. "Complete, peaceful, thankful. Needless."

"Reassured, welcoming. Departing reconnect. Farewell."

"Farewell."

That was it for three days, nine words from the total population of the planet then, perhaps, another nine when leaving. It was normal to them, yet his mind could not conceive a life built on nine words a week, two of which were required ritualistic salutations. They'd hardly used more when they let him know his brother died.

He resumed his outward gaze, the world now a flowing yellow river as the autodrive sped on. Perhaps here nine were enough, maybe even too many. Yellow. Boring. Lumpy. They were enough to describe the land flowing past him, sufficient to encompass it all and leave the listener with few doubts, no real questions. Add in cold, warm, night and day and the whole ecosystem could be covered. He'd seen no other living thing, plant or animal, since his arrival. An ocean, land and the one hundred of the Brotherhood. The planet in total. Perhaps it had never been given a name as there was hardly anything worth calling. Planet. A place described in its entirety by eight words, perhaps nine if 'rock' was added, the only thing he could see in abundance. Of all places it was here, fifty years ago, his brother had come to, lived, and died four months earlier. For all that he'd never spared one word, let alone nine, for Gordon, his mother or his family. Until the Prelate spoke for him, of his death to Gordon, his only blood left alive, and from that the choice to come was a simple one, a chance to see what could so completely contain his brother. While he was alive no such contact was permissible; once Jules had passed a brief window opened to him, one Gordon would not miss.

Their last words were on his departure, a bright day on their green azure world waiting for the train to take Jules away. Cocksure and nineteen Gordon's world had been shaken by Jules' announcement. Twelve years older and an accomplished physicist it was a seismic blow, one no one had time to accept or rationalize.

"A hermit? It's one thing to get religion but shutting yourself off like that's crazy."

His brother had smiled at him, a half-pitying half-amused grin. It wasn't quite smugness, and it was easy to see sadness underneath.

"It's not for everyone. It's necessary, necessary for my faith."

"Faith? You're a man of science Jules, it's not the Dark Ages. Faith in what, a god that does what science can't explain today but will tomorrow?"

"You know it's not that, no 'god of the gaps' or such rubbish. And don't be so quick to ridicule faith, some would say science is just a different religion."

"I don't think so!"

"You'd better believe it. Everything in science is based on assumptions, simplifications, events or processes taken as granted and given and not necessarily observed. You tell me that's not faith, faith of a different kind but faith nonetheless."

He laughed, reached down and moved his face closer, grinning broadly.

"Don't forget Gordo, you're training to be an economist and if there's anything based on faith and presumption that is."

The last call for his train came and too quickly Jules was gone, lost in the crowd. My last words to my brother a stupid argument over the irrelevant.

The autodrive started to make its way through a series of switchbacks, climbing slowly as the land opened up to a vast plain. I could see the glint of steel where my slipship sat, the land now an elongated waffle, maple syrup patterns gently resting on yellow batter.

Jules had been right. Economics was simplifying assumption loaded upon simplifying assumption until it was broadly applicable to something, specifically applicable to nothing. People reduced to response-stimuli factors and bell curve residents, flatly refusing to obey the gods of demand and supply until in fits of rationalist anger and determinative despair Keynes's six-hundred year old ghost gets dragged from its cloister and his 'animal spirits' trotted out yet again to explain the unexplainable. The harder I threw myself at economics the less I understood it; the more knowledge I gained, the less I knew about anything; until gazing down the hill of old age I understood the only thing I didn't know was everything. And there my brother stood, half-pitying, half-amused grin on his face, having got there a half century before me.

We'd reached a plateau, the autodrive speeding along the yellow ribbon towards the edge, me staring alternately to the right to a small range of mountains just making themselves known on the horizon, then to the valley floor on the left bathed in early afternoon sun. My feelings shifted slightly, some of the boring had shaken off as the landscape glimmered in the sunlight, gently swaying arms of brown waving at me. Perhaps a little solitude, a little peace and quiet was called for, might do me some good. Not that I had desires towards being a hermit or locking myself away in isolation, I'd just become a touch selective about my surroundings, human or otherwise. Knowing that I really knew nothing instantly made those that thought they did grate on me, intentional or not, and I'd found myself actively avoiding the twenty and thirty somethings that resembled a younger I. I started to understand my elders' quiet not to be acquiescence or acceptance, but rather a melancholy rejection of the lives they'd lived. Faith, as Jules had maintained, is not changed but rather what it is placed in shifts.

I cracked the roof open a touch, inviting a raucous whistle of cold, a heavily scented jumble of vanilla and magnolia sweeping over me that couldn't exist here yet by its very presence mocked the thought. The ridge narrowed, swung to the right. The autodrive headed towards one growing peak, an ocean of pale green closing in welcome from the left. With a little effort I could look down, see line after small line of pea-froth breakers railing against a shore of deep yellow, crashing upslope then falling back one after the other. In vain I looked for the seabirds, grasses and shells that littered the beaches at home; here there were none, the mother ocean barren or choosing not to cast her life onto dry land to prosper, the emptiness of yellow brown melding with the emptiness of pale green.

The coldness of the air and the heavy laden scents it bore conspired with the rhythm of tires on packed gravel and warming afternoon sun to lull me into a reflective mood. It hadn't made much sense to me, why the Brotherhood would chose this far-flung rock rather than an established, populated world that surely would have posed fewer problems, simpler logistics, but chose it they had and in its entirety it was theirs. That, along with some small scraps gleaned here and there represented my entire knowledge of the group. How you became a brother was a paradox in itself. The only way to find out the requirements and definitions was to become a Brother; the only way to become a Brother was to meet the requirements and definitions.

Some small fragments started to make sense to me, their reliance on the old documents for one. My life, as for trillions like me, was one of previously unimagined richness and fulfillment, an all-embracing dance of challenge and reward, logic and emotion cocooned in the breast of technology, a cosmos-wide ocean of connection, information, support and interaction. A life from cradle to the grave shared, but not quite in its entirety, with everyone, differences notable yet muted enough to allow variety without discrimination, genius without megalomania, passion without fanaticism. Yet an unimaginably small fraction rejected it and the all-encompassing society in various ways and for diverse alternatives, always radical, usually violent, mainly ego driven narcissism. Those in the Brotherhood had simply left, and although their numbers never grew beyond the hundred yet did they never fall below.

Always, it seemed, as one died another came to take their place.

They never claimed to be modern luddites, simply the pendulum for them had swung too far. To express their desires they drew from the ancient texts, in particular one from the dawn of time when Earth itself was barely populated and humanity only one step removed from the apes. 'The world today is sick to its thin blood for lack of elemental things,' the heartfelt call lamented 'for fire before the hands, for water welling from the earth, for air, for the dear earth itself underfoot'. Now, with the mesmeric landscape and unfamiliar silence in and around me I felt drawn slightly closer to their minds, their perspective.

We approached the crest of the isthmus, the ocean to my left a now familiar pea green, that to my right deep olive and wind driven, the waves crashing against the near vertical cliffs of dull yellow, climbing fissures in soaring columns to fall back in misty disappointment. We drew near a single peak standing proud on the promontory, a solitary landmark before the ocean claimed the horizon. Behind me the isthmus fell away to join the plateau spreading left and right, the plains running away to the horizon; I had climbed the back of a giant prostrate dragon of yellow-brown.

The road ended part way up the peak, the autodrive shutting down as I alighted. A series of steps spiraled up the peak ending in a small landing. The crest was hidden from view, a room or rooms within betrayed by a faint blue-white glow against the rapidly darkening sky. A silhouetted figure gazed silently down from the landing. I pulled my collar closer, shifted my grip onto my shoulder, and made my way up.

Even after fifty years the figure was recognizable. I stood quietly, regarding it carefully.

"Been a long time Jules."

"You're looking good Gordo. How long've I been dead?"

"Just on four months."

The simulacra held out his hands, carefully studied the nails, then turned them over and repeated the examination on his palms.

"Not bad, one day, perhaps two before death I'd say. Always was meticulous."

"Do you mind if we continue this indoors? It's getting cold."

"Yes, yes, sure. I'm sorry, I forget I don't notice anymore."

We stepped through a doorway to a small room carved from the yellow-brown rock. Austere and slightly warmer than outside it held a chair, a hat stand and a solitary dim bulb swinging above the polished floor. There was just enough room for both of us to stand.

"Seems a bit on the tiny side even for a monk's cell."

"What? Oh this! No, it's just the cloakroom. Here, give me your coat."

I handed it to him and it fell straight through his outstretched hand. He smiled, slightly abashed.

"Oh, I should remember shouldn't I? Looks like old habits die hard. Could you …?"

"Yeah, sure."

I picked my coat up and hung it on the stand, placed my grip on the floor below it. A doorway appeared and I followed Jules through.

It was no palace but it was far from the bare habitation I'd expected. A circular room with domed roof, glass extended around and through it providing unobstructed views across the surrounding oceans, the plains behind and the now emerging stars above. On one side a half flight of stairs led to a mezzanine floor jutting out away from the plains, a room of glass hovering above the cliff face below, a low bed, heavily laden bookcase and small rug clearly visible through the transparent floor. Next to an ablutions alcove was a small kitchen area if one could call a shelf, solitary hotplate and spigot any such thing. Two chairs, small coffee table, desk, an open fireplace and clothes chest completed the room's furnishings. The room appeared to have been carved out of the peak, the interior colored by bands of yellows and browns running diagonally across the floor, walls and ceiling, broken irregularly by random flecks of blue, opalescent rock. The room shone, polished bright by design or ages of inhabitation reflecting the pale light from wall strips back on itself then out to the night.

I moved to a pair of inlaid glass doors on the far side, noticing a distinct if subtle bowing in the stone floor. Steps led down from the doors to a large walled terraced garden, the shapes of trees and smaller plants visible in the pale blue-white glow. It was the only life

I had seen on the planet, and it briefly held me.

"You like my garden?"

"Yes, it's unexpected."

"They grow well here, surprising really. Descendants of the original seed stock I'm told, we each have one, just enough to keep body together."

He turned with a sigh, headed towards the nearest chair.

"Started to get too much for me in the end, all those stairs with these knees."

He hesitated before sitting, reconsidered and placed himself carefully down on an adjacent hard backed chair.

"Please, make yourself comfortable Gordo."

I did as asked, sinking just enough into the cushions to feel at home. The silence, the simple yet cozy room nestled in its faint light wrapped in a thousand stars relaxed me, made me feel welcomed. It was a room I could easily be comfortable in, for a while, even with self-imposed solitude. It had been a long few days and I fought to keep my eyes open.

"Why Gordo?"

"Why what?"

"Why'd you come here, make the effort?"

"To see, maybe get a few answers."

"It was too late when they told you."

He spread his palms outwards.

"Is this going to be enough?"

"It's more than I've had in fifty years, it'll do."

We sat in silence observing each other, two old men trying to reconcile the figures before them to their last meeting. I tried, unsuccessfully, to stifle a yawn.

Jules stood, embarrassed.

"Of course, you must be tired. Perhaps rest first, we can talk tomorrow. I think you know where everything is, just call me when you're ready." with which Jules winked off.

"Goodnight Jules." I whispered to the empty room. I took myself and my grip to the mezzanine, settled onto the bed. A small box wrapped in brown paper at the end of the bed caught my eye.

'Gordo, From Jules' was written neatly on the wrapping. He

must have done this before he died, must have known he was dying and I would come, placing it here for me. I unwrapped it, lifted the lid, then just stared at the contents. A simple carbon-fiber chain ended in a small, obsidian black polished stone no larger than my thumbnail. At its center, shimmering iridescent orange, turquoise and yellow was a sliver of lodestone. I'd seen paintings, heard the myths, even dreamed the dreams everyone seemed to have about them, but to actually have one? No one knew where they originated. Wisdom, longevity, even the mind of god some said could be had through them. Only those who had one could say for sure, and they had not.

I moved my fingers closer until they were nearly touching it. I felt a fire course through my arm, the room recede in a blur of light as I flew upwards and out, a chorus of welcoming voices calling for me, urging me on as the universe tried to find its way into my head. I pulled my arm away as if stung, looking down at the lodestone, shaken. I put the lid back on the box and the box in turn in the bottom of my grip. One more question to add to the list for tomorrow.

I couldn't recall the last time I'd woken to just the sun, aroused without alarm or cajoling to get up, get out and run the corporate treadmill. The gentle warming, caressing fingers of light making their way over the foot of the bed slowly pried my eyes open to bring me into the day rested, not resentful. I left Jules off, made my way down the stairs to the garden. Leaving my sandals behind I allowed myself the walk across the grass, massaging my soles on the dewless blades. I sat on the low stone wall, legs dangling out above the precipice, yellow-blue sun warming me slowly. Devoid of life perhaps, but regardless the oceans in front of me burst with activity. The two waters met before me, a line of bubbling sworls stretching out to the horizon as pea green on the left met olive to my right. Far out near the horizon they sent their waves in, crashing together in foaming green striped silence until closer in and strength dissipated the mid-green amalgam reached the shallows and, once more invigorated, rose in vain to tilt at the rocks below, the sounds of clashes between they and the unrelenting cliff rising to meet me, the only ears within a thousand kilometers.

High tide coming perhaps, and no sooner had I thought it than the moon popped up above the horizon, a small, dull pewter affair with nothing to commend further examination, a pale imitation of the moons surrounding home. A pleasant place perhaps for contemplation, yet how long until this would fall to banal normality? I turned, made my way back inside.

I busied myself after a quick breakfast with a closer examination of the room, hoping to gain an understanding of at least part of Jules' life before we next talked. A forlorn hope carried through in vain, the room yielding no hints, no clues. Bare and sparse it seemed and bare and sparse it was, no personal items beyond some clothes, a few well-worn books, and the box left for me on the bed. Oddly there were no religious texts, human or otherwise to be found, no iconography on the walls, crucifixes or symbols surrounding the room. It was as if my brother was at a hotel or boarding house, his possessions and effects at home while he traveled for the briefest of stays, never intending to remain. But wasn't that the point, the core of the decision he'd made those years ago? I laughed, made sure my coffee was hot, and sat down.

"Good morning Jules."

He appeared where he had left last night.

"Gordo, I trust you slept well?"

"I did, thank you. And you?" I kicked myself as I said it.

He cocked his head to one side, wide eyed.

"Like the dead, thank you."

It was a short, strained silence that followed, one I was both eager to break and atone for.

"Thank you for the present, you didn't have to."

"What present?"

"The one on the bed, upstairs, brown paper wrapped box."

"I can't remember doing that."

"Surely you couldn't forget giving a lodestone away?"

His face lit up.

"Ah, perhaps I did after I'd made this copy. I take it you don't have it on right now?"

"Perhaps later, not yet. It's a little … overpowering."

Jules reached below the folds of his vest, pulled out a lodestone, the twin of the one now sitting in my grip.

"Yes, at first they are, but one quickly becomes used to it." He saw my surprise. "Oh yes, it's one for each of the Brotherhood, a normal part of the faith you could say."

He held it briefly in front of him, then placed it back inside his vest.

"But that's merely an aside, you didn't come here to see my jewelry."

I wondered how to start the conversation, how to be adult about it and not appear to whine or blame. I'd practiced unsuccessfully on the journey, remonstrating with myself over the stupidity of trying not to hurt a simulacra's feelings while simultaneously understanding it was my feelings I was hoping to leave intact. I was still no closer to a solution so, as was more and more frequently happening to me, age and pure bloody-mindedness won out.

"I'm all that's left Jules, all there's been for ages. I need some answers, maybe closure before it's my turn."

He sat on the wooden chair.

"Oh, I see."

"You left in such a hurry, we couldn't understand why. You never gave much of an explanation to mum, you know she never stopped lighting those damned candles for you, twenty years she did at that cathedral, Saint whatsits ..."

"Celia's."

"Yes, Saint Celia's. You never let her know you were safe, not one word. Why? You knew she couldn't come here."

"You know I couldn't, it's the Orders, contact outside the Brotherhood is forbidden, it diverts us, clouds mind, purpose and vision."

"But couldn't you spare two words, even one just to let her know? She died wondering, hoping you were fine but wondering, it wasn't right or fair."

"It couldn't be helped, even thinking about the past wasn't allowed. Once that lodestone went around my neck, once the Brotherhood accepted me, I ceased to exist outside it, everything changed. Even now, even as a simulacra it's hard to change that habit."

"Would it have been so hard, just to leave a little slower, not just rush off?"

"I had a … timeline … to stick to. If I'd stayed a week a month or a year would it really have helped? What's crueler, death by a thousand cuts or one swipe of the blade?"

Perhaps he was right, and if the finger pointing and arguing after he had gone was any measure he was definitely right.

"I missed having you there, you know, just being there. There were times I needed you."

"You turned out ok though didn't you?"

"Yes, but it was close, real close."

"You really didn't need me, I'm not sure anyone did. For what it's worth if I made your or anyone's life harder I'm sorry but I wouldn't change it. You know what I was like, I never made rash decisions but once my mind's made up there's no point hanging around, just get on with it. Don't forget it cost me too."

"Dee?"

"Of course."

There were two stunned families when he left, mine and his. A wife of three years, thankfully no children. I'd been left to pick up the pieces.

"She said you never told her about it."

"I said as much as I could, to her and anyone, as much as I was able."

"You left it to me to deal with as well as our family. She had no one else you know, no one at all."

"What happened to her?"

"How do I know? Anyway it's too late now."

He leant back, dropped his head down above steepled fingers. It was a convincing simulacra, right down to the movement and inflections. He raised his eyes to me mimicking that big brother pose of a lifetime ago.

"Gordo, cut to the chase. You're too old for games and I'm beyond it. If you came here to try and load guilt on me it's not going to work, this isn't me you know that. Anyway, I had to work all that through decades ago. You said you wanted answers well tell me, what is it you really want?"

The sun had risen to its zenith following a long low arc across the southern sky. The light fell through the windows as luminous shafts, dust motes dancing around each other as the sun warmed and the shadows cooled. Once the sun had set there would be no more dancing. My time here was nearly over, tomorrow the journey home.

"Did you find it?"

"What?"

"The answer, god, faith, what you came here for."

"How long have the doctors given you?"

"How do you know?"

"How long Gordo? Months, weeks?"

"Five, maybe six months if I do what they say."

"You're scared."

"Of course, why wouldn't I be? No one wants to die and I don't. Intellectually I know it's inevitable but that's no help. Nothing else helps, it's all just fables and tales no one can explain, never mind prove."

"I found it Gordo."

He had an air of certainty, absolute finality about him. Not fanatical conviction but a quiet, deep certitude.

"You found god?"

"No, not what you think. I'm not even sure god exists. I found something else, something far, far better, a way to outlive my body, my diseases. A gift, an invitation made to few."

He reached into his vest, pulled the lodestone out.

"This is what I came for, what I found, what will preserve me."

"The lodestone?"

"Exactly. What do you know about them?"

"Nothing, just the stories. Only a few of them exist, no one knows where they come from but they give knowledge and power to whoever has one, makes them nearly divine."

"This one's obviously not real. Can you go and bring the real one down?"

I retrieved it, placing it down safely nestled in its box where I couldn't accidentally touch it. Jules was smiling gently, concentrating.

"Take the lid off, I would but, you know."

The sliver was no longer iridescent but glowing, sending a rainbow colored halo of light spilling over the edges of the box. Beautiful was not enough, transcendent came close.

Jules leant forwards to touch it then, as if thinking better of it, slowly settled back in his chair.

"Some call it the 'Eye of God' or the 'Almighty's Heart'. It's neither and more, much more than you could imagine. The rarest jewel in the universe, that's the myth. What you don't know is how rare, there are only one hundred and twenty five of these."

"One for each one in the Brotherhood?"

"And twenty-five over, twenty-five selected individuals. None of them own them, they are simply gifted for life. Always on loan, always come back when the borrower translates, always back out again."

"So it pays for all of this?"

"This and more, far more. Our safety, isolation, privacy. Absolute and total."

"And you own them all?"

"No, we're merely custodians. No one owns them, no one can. And it's not really them, it's only one lodestone, one in a hundred and twenty-six places at once, scattered across the universe."

"You said there were only one hundred twenty-five."

"Yes, slivers that is. Come with me."

Jules stood, moved to the kitchen. I followed, the sliver sat in its box in the middle of the room glowing, the rainbow halo spilling out across the table. Jules pointed to a flat panel above his head.

"Put your hand here. It's DNA coded so it'll work for you."

I reached up, placed my hand flat against it. It glowed a faint green, a gentle hiss from the middle of the room startling me. I turned, following Jules' gaze.

Cracks appeared in the floor, one enclosing the coffee table, a second encircling the room lying close by my feet. Between them an iris opened, coffee table at the center, Jules and I on the edge, a gaping chasm between. The sliver burned, a column of incandescent light rising to the roof then cascading back down the walls, down through the cavern. It was to me an afterthought, lost detail in what was now below me.

I couldn't see the bottom of the chasm, couldn't see across it. Something stood in the middle nearly filling the void, following the walls down as far as I could see. It burned, an incomprehensible explosion of light and color flaming outwards and through me, from not a sliver, not a rock, but a mountain of lodestone at my feet. The universe erupted from it, returned, exploded coursing through me in a continuous cycle of birth, death, regeneration each different, each the same. In the middle of it all the siren call of millions of voices begging me, encouraging me, demanding me, and at the center one voice above all loud and clear. Jules.

It was overwhelming, shattering in its intensity. My hand fell from the panel, the iris folding back returning the floor to normality, the sliver resuming its gentle halo. I sank down against the wall in a shivering, cold sweat, Jules beside me.

"There's one hundred of these dwellings across this world, each with one of the Brotherhood, each with a sliver. Each dwelling has that beneath it, one arm reaching out from the core of the planet."

He looked across the room, to the gently glowing sliver.

"One entity, an entire planet twelve thousand kilometers wide, one hundred arms poking up through six hundred kilometers of shale and sand to the surface. We didn't find It, It found us. You've noticed nothing living on the surface, just us and our gardens?"

"Yes."

"Way back before we swung out of the trees there was a civilization here, people with interstellar flight. They sent out the slivers It gave them. They were the ones who started the Brotherhood millennia ago."

"What happened to them?"

"What always happens, the civilization died out but there's a difference, a big difference. Some of them still live Gordo, and will forever absorbed, joined with It before they died. Chosen, accepting, voluntary merging. You know why?"

He didn't let me get a word in.

"Because It's eternal Gordo, It started when time itself started and will keep on when time itself has died. It knows how the universe started, knows how it will end, and It's making sure life will come to the new one, and the one after that, and the one after that, eternally. Each sliver, each of the hundred and twenty-five is with someone who will join with us, someone who will be part of this cycle, the next cycle, all cycles. While they live they're linked to the conscious collective mind, using the wisdom and knowledge of millennia, and when they die to be joined, merged. Not random picks, not the rich or powerful that myth says, but carefully and painstakingly chosen. By us."

"Selected?"

"What do you think the Brotherhood does, what I did for the past fifty years? It's our prime purpose, under all the silence and solitude and separation. We cull, we trawl through the quadrillions of sentient beings in the universe looking, reaching out and identifying the next ones, the two or three each year that are ready and suitable to carry it through, the chosen, ones like us."

"Like you, you mean?"

"Yes, like me. I was chosen, like we all were. Me by Dee's father. He was called the year Dee was born, and he called me fifty years ago, when I was ready. Here, in this room I joined. And now I'm calling you. We want you to join us."

"You're offering me eternal life?"

"No, we are, me, It and the others chosen over millennia joined below us. You're ready, you're right and the time is right. There's always a small door, a few months or weeks when a candidate is suitable. For me I had two weeks, just two weeks. You, five months. Five months after I chose to join, to merge with It. After that it's not possible."

"You expect me to believe you'd suicide to give me eternal life?"

"No, I know you believe it, I know it's what called you here, no mere desire to see where I spent my life or get any 'closure', but our call. You might not have seen me for these years but we've been watching you, working towards this one moment."

He was right of course, I knew he was right and what was on offer was real, not the pipe-dream of a dying old man.

"So what do I do?"

"Tomorrow you make a choice. You either send your ship back without you, or you go home. If you go home you will never have the offer made again. If you just put the necklace on, hang that sliver round your neck, you're part of the Brotherhood, eternal life with me, the others."

"That simple?"

"Yes, that simple. The choice is yours."

He stood, looking down as he'd done decades ago.

"Well that's it, I've done what I was asked to do. I'd shake your hand but, well, that's a useless gesture."

I stood beside him. He moved his face closer, his nose nearly touching mine, wicked grin on his face.

"It's been fun Gordo. Make the right choice and I'll see you tomorrow." With which he winked off permanently.

I didn't sleep that night, forced myself not to make a rash choice, to be swayed by losing my brother a second time or the chance to regain him. It seemed clear, an opportunity humanity had dreamt of, built kingdoms and religions around, and all I had to do was put a sliver of lodestone around my neck. I gazed at the box as I sat on the bed, the small halo not falling haphazardly but now a clear, beckoning finger of light aimed at me. An inviting yet mildly sinister sight from which I could not draw my eyes away. One act to be joined to millions of minds, selecting those to spend eternity with, to shape the universes to come. Another act to accept mortality, join the countless trillions in non-existence, testament to the quiet desperation and silent despair of ordinary life.

I was locked in thought as the autodrive took me to my slipship, back through a landscape now familiar yet arrogant, apart. There was no way to send my ship back remotely, the autos had to be set by hand.

I tried to imagine the planet teeming with life, reaching out to the stars to search for intellect, for individuals deemed worthy to carry life forward. I tried to grasp the selection of one out of billions, an untold number winnowed without knowing. I could not.

I put them all in front of me, my parents, Dee, my wives, my children and grandchildren, friends and enemies, imagining them dust while I lived on. Would they curse me or bless me? Envy or hate? Would they trade places, move to godhood while I perished?

Did it even matter?

The autodrive came to a halt, my slipship opening for me. I clambered inside, set the necessary processes in motion, resumed my seat.

"Audio only. Prelate."

"Prelate connected. Continue." the autodrive announced.

"Eternal. Thankful."

"Eternal indeed. Resolution?"

"Declined. Grateful. Departing."

"Sadness. Farewell."

The planet shimmered slightly below me, lemon on velvet popping out of sight as the slipship drive engaged. I relaxed, bought up the newsfeed and settled into the trip home.

END

SUICIDE IS NOT ENOUGH

SHE WAS STONE, with none of the histrionics, tears or emotion that mark the fault lines of a crumbling marriage. The earth had split asunder soundlessly, deliberately, and nothing would heal the breach. After making sure their son was safely buckled in Pat turned, wound down the window.

"Its taken years but you've convinced me Aaron. You're a loser, a waste of my time and everyone else's. Don't try to find me, don't call, it's over."

The car drove slowly away from 5 Rose Lane. She didn't spare him a backwards glance, closing curtains all that greeted him as the neighborhood gossips hid as he went inside.

The kitchen table was no friendlier. A pile of final demands and bills competed with another of rejections, both put to shame by foreclosure notices. At least it would make property settlement easier, half of nothing is nothing. This time next month it would be all over, nothing left, no prospects, just a litany of failure. The only thing left was to wipe his life from the face of the earth.

He glared at his pills. Three failures proved they couldn't do it. How a whole bottle couldn't kill you was beyond him, beyond even the paramedics claiming it was a miracle he was alive. Assholes.

He shrugged on his coat, walked out leaving the door swinging. He gave the finger to Mrs. Rosendahl as he turned the corner, he couldn't see her but he knew the old bat was always watching, sniping, gossiping.

Aaron wandered aimlessly until he found himself staring at a simple plaque announcing the office of Erasure Inc. He laughed. At least my subconscious is working properly. He pushed the door open and made his way up the narrow flight of stairs. A small, balding man bearing an uncanny resemblance to a large rat greeted him.

"Hello, I'm Johann Renck, manager. You can call me Johann if you like mister …?"

He stared at the outstretched hand, unwilling to take it.

"Kelly, Aaron Kelly."

"Mr. Kelly, yes. Please take a seat."

Johann sat down delicately. The office was as plain and dour as the man.

"So you wish to use our services?"

"Yes, I've read your … offering on the net. It's really totally painless, you've had no complaints?"

"Absolutely. It's not the sort of business where customers can complain Mr. Kelly."

"How much, I mean, the cost, I couldn't see what it was."

"There is none, it's free. Money's quite irrelevant really, we can't actually take any payment."

"Why?"

"The … process … makes it quite impossible, quite impossible. But don't worry for the business Mr. Kelly, we receive payment for everyone we help so we aren't impoverished."

"And the rest, free too?"

"Part of the service we are proud to offer of course."

"How can you —"

"Ah now Mr. Kelly, if everyone knew where would my business be? In any case I will be happy to tell you when the process commences, if you decide to go ahead."

"I'm decided, I want to go with it as early as possible."

"Very good. Let me check. Jenny!"

A woman, his twin in appearance and dress, stepped in and handed Johann a tablet. He scrolled quickly, made a hurried note on the back of a business card and handed it to Aaron.

"Thursday, ten a.m. Does that work for you?"

Aaron stood, offered his hand.

"Yes, perfectly. Thursday it is."

"Excellent. No food or drink for twelve hours beforehand please Mr. Kelly, we must minimize the physical after effects."

Pat carefully placed the china cup on the saucer and smiled. Aaron may never have liked his mother but by some strange quirk she got along famously with Pat. He might not visit but she did every Thursday morning. Kid at school, work on hold for a few hours it was pleasant enough.

"So it's over?"

"Yes, Tuesday morning. Aaron's not said?"

"No Pat, he hasn't and I wouldn't expect him too. He might be my own flesh and blood but I know an idiot when I see one. I thought maybe he'd improve with you but it's not the way things went."

"I thought kids might have helped, maybe marriage, but honestly Dot he's a lost cause."

"At least you're free of him dear."

He closed his eyes waiting for the first punch. The Ryan kids kept at him all morning about his dad and mum splitting. Shoulda ignored them but I didn't, now it's gonna hurt.

A hand wrenched his arm from his face. Jake started to shake, the school bully towering over him.

"I'm not thumping you Jake."

"Whatcha gonna do Ted?"

"Nuthin', just like nobody else."

Ted scowled at the circle of kids, grabbed Jake by the shoulders and half guided, half pulled him to the school gate.

"Let's have some fun."

Jake followed as Ted vaulted the low chain-wire fence and walked towards the mall.

"My parents split too, so if they're gonna pick on you they'll hafta pick on me."

Roxy lifted the trowel, twisted it a half turn then chopped the potting mix back into the planter. She straightened, took one step back and sat down. It may be only two bedrooms on the fifth floor but a south facing apartment in the city's a good thing. I'd wanted a house, a decent yard to grow and plant but we just missed out.

I really don't like living in the city, the flat's good but I can't relax, I never feel comfortable walking down the road Clay died on, the signs of the hit and run still etched into the brickwork and steel. You'd think after time the pain would ease, perhaps just a little.

The gurney was comfortable. Johann fussed over a few small wires, handed him a small glass of clear liquid.

"A relaxant, nothing more. Just helps our machine do its job. Your last chance, go or no go. Drink it and we'll proceed."

Aaron drained the glass in one swallow. Slightly aniseed, sweet.

"So, we begin. Everything is automatic now, when it's time the machine will send you into a gentle sleep, do its work and that's that. I believe I said I'd explain it to you. Do you still want me to?"

Aaron felt tipsy, slightly high. Explanation? Why not.

"Sure, but keep it simple, time is money."

"Indeed it is, indeed it is. It's very simple Mr. Kelly. The machine is a failed experiment, my failed experiment, one of the old DARPA time travel boondoggles. As far as they could figure it was a disaster. No travel, just destruction, cancellation. It was a failure so, naturally, I was too. You know what they say Mr. Kelly, success has a thousand fathers, failure's an orphan. So I changed it, just a little, and here I am."

He tapped Aaron gently on the headband.

"This tunes the machine to you, your fingerprint in time. It traces you all the way back from when it starts the process to the moment you were conceived. As it's doing that, as a side-effect really, it erases each and every point from your timeline until, literally, you have never existed and never did."

"And then? At the end?"

"I won't remember you; you won't remember you; no one will. All there will be is a lump of flesh, a shell that is nothing."

He turned, moved to the screen on the desk.

"It's why we can't charge you. You could give us the money but that will be erased, written over and reset. It's just a minor, unnecessary complication. Are you ready?"

"Born ready."

"Goodbye Mr. Kelly."

A small jolt through his head sent Aaron into a pleasant, waking dream. Happy, relaxed, totally unable to move he was watching the movie of his life spool backwards slowly, but with gathering pace. His eyes closed, breath shallow, all sense of the room left him.

Maybe, just maybe Pat and I can manage, can get through it, I've got to try just that bit harder, be more positive and thorough.

"So you're still arguing, still shouting?"

"Yes, sometimes Dot but we're trying to at least get him more positive."

"We tried for years his father and I, a lifetime but we couldn't even scratch the surface."

"The wedding seems to have helped."

"It's early days yet Pat."

"You like Doom?"

A brace of daemons exploded as Jake let off another rpg.

"Yeah, never played it on this big a screen tho'. My dad's got it on Xbox but we only have a small tv."

"Least your dad's home, mine's always out with my aunties. Mum says they're his girlfriends, they keep shouting."

A horned beast jumped up, a quick swipe of a chainsaw finishing it off.

"Mine keep throwin' and breakin' stuff, then dad just cries in the kitchen all night."

"Stupid parents."

"You bet."

Carol looked over her coffee at Roxy.

"How long you lived here?"

"Two, maybe three years."

"Seriously, you need to get out more, enjoy it. Past's past Roxy, Clay wouldn't want you sad."

"I know, I know. Still hard though."

The spirit level never lies but there's no requirement to believe it. Clearly the mailbox was not straight but it was rapid set concrete and it was on his land. His land. All that mattered. A house, a kid and a woman. Aaron smiled. They'd nearly been outbid by that other couple but that little extra push and now it was theirs.

He stood, stretched, and looked out from 5 Rose Lane over his domain. Roots. Roots make the difference, keep the tree grounded, and now he had them. Roots. A home. Maybe this would do it.

"So maybe a wedding later, now you've your own home?"

Pat laughed, took another sip of tea.

"Maybe. Perhaps. He seems happier but we've managed ok without one up to now Dot."

"I'm sure many young couples do these days, quite sure."

"You're lucky."

The aliens melted as Jake sprayed acid over them.

"Huh?"

"You gotta house and all, I'm still in the van park."

"I guess."

"No guess, I wish I had my own room."

"You coming or what?"

Clay looked back, laughing as Roxy tried to balance her handbag and jacket in one hand while fiddling with her shoe with the other.

"Wait up a bit, I don't know this city like you."

He took her jacket in one hand, steadied her with the other.

"Now just take your time. We can take a shortcut down the alleyway, it's narrow but we'll get there on time."

"Can't we stick to the sidewalk?"

"And miss the show? Hell no! If you're gonna live in the city you might as well learn to enjoy it."

She jumped him right at half time, five foot eight of brunette straddling him like a prize bull. She wrapped her arms around his neck, dragged his face closer until their noses touched, gave him a lascivious grin.

"Children."

"What?"

"Children now Aaron."

"But you said —"

Pat switched the tv off and threw the remote away.

"That was yesterday. Now is now."

"Are you sure?"

She threw him down on the couch.

"Positive."

"My son seems quite serious about you Patricia."

"Please, call me Pat. And yes, we've been together for a while now."

"And you must call me Dot, none of that 'Mrs. Kelly' nonsense. He's talked a lot about you but honestly there's nothing better than actually meeting you."

"I'm glad I could drop over, Thursday mornings always seem easier for me to get time from work."

"Oh, why?"

"Stock filling Thursday mornings, not much I can do without the consumables."

He hated playing by himself but hated school and the other kids more. The teachers didn't care, just like mum and dad they seemed happier when he wasn't around.

None of the other kids understood, no one else had parents who always shouted, hit each other, hit him, stayed away nights with other people then went soft and soppy on him.

His soldier died, last of his lives gone. Top score again. The screen flashed for his name. 'T – E – D – 0 – 1" he put in.

Shame there was no one to see it.

Clay filled the cups slowly. With one arm around Roxy he looked out from the front veranda of 5 Rose Lane. Another peaceful Thursday morning at home.

"Carnations."

"What?"

"Carnations honey, I think we need carnations. Maybe reds."

Roxy nodded, placed her cup down.

"And yellows, don't forget the yellows."

She was out of his league and if his inner voice wasn't enough his friends were there to remind him. The dance floor seemed miles wide, boys round one edge, girls the other. He was committed, the dare accepted and no way out. He walked haltingly forwards, a lone figure heading to the unknown. He stopped in front of her.

"Ah, I'm, ah … hello, do you want to ah …"

She grabbed him by the hand, smiling, led him away.

"Dance Aaron? Yes, about time you asked."

"I'm sorry. I really can't remember."

They stood in the doorway, the old lady and the young staring in amusement at each other.

"Well let's say it's an old woman's mind going. Once I remember I'll get in touch. What was your name again?"

"Patricia, Patricia Jenkins."

"Well Miss Jenkins, it's been a pleasure … I think."

"Same here Mrs. …"

"Kelly, Dorothy Kelly."

It was all loud and interesting, sometimes scary, some things happened again and again. There was that shape, the one that was there when he fed, it was a smell and a feel that was familiar, comforting. As he fell asleep it would make soft noises, as he woke it would slowly brush itself against him. It felt safe, smooth.

Then the other one, the one that felt not smooth, that was louder. It didn't have milk, it didn't make soft noises when he grew tired, it wasn't there when the soft shape was here. It was here now, making hard noises.

"You little shit, if I had my way youd've been aborted. You chained me here, ruined my life, I hate you."

Traffic was light for a weekday, she'd make it easily for midday.

Another Thursday morning window shopping, coffee for one and not much else. A simple life uncluttered by others Pat was reasonably happy. Or at least not sad.

The clock struck twelve, chimed, then continued on its way to one o'clock. Dot regarded it coldly, cursing its echoing through the empty house. What's the point of marking empty hours in an empty life, reminders of what wasn't and isn't? No family, no friends, just time.

The bell chimed.

"Another one?"

"Seems so Jenny."

They walked into the room. A man lay on the gurney vacant eyed, drooling. At least this one hadn't soiled itself. He pulled the surgical gown off exposing a small tattoo on the left breast.

"Jake. Hmm. Hello whoever you are, welcome to the rest of your life. Jenny, I'll call Forma if you'll prep him."

She moved her gaze from the man's groin.

"A bit of a waste."

"Well you've missed your chance, he's not good for anything now."

He turned to the door. Jenny laughed, called after him.

"You're not going to help? Getting squeamish?"

"You would too, the food and air lines are one thing but watching the catheter insertions still gives me the creeps."

Pat changed into her lab coat, pushed through the swing doors. Erica was at the far end of the room starting prep. Products still need to be tested, reactions gauged even if animal cruelty laws were enforced. Well we'll never run foul of them again.

"Hey Erica, how many?"

"Just the one, good subject though."

"Plugged and ready?"

"Uh huh, prised and strapped. What are we running?"

Pat crossed the room, looked down.

"See what you mean, we might get six months out of this one."

She turned, picked up her clipboard.

"Ok, series five and six, chemical toxin irritants skin and eyes for J.D.J. Rips and drips Erica."

She looked at the test subject. His skin was clean, eyes bright if a touch weepy, near perfect. Only one small flaw but that was easily worked around. She snapped on her rubber gloves, stepped back.

"Welcome to Forma Jake. I promise this will hurt a great deal."

END

LESSON

JAKE YANCY'S PARENTS, like all parents, were happy and scared when their small bundle of joy arrived. They did their best as best they could, squeezing him into their busy lives between work, sleep, friends and Netflix. Like most they won some and lost some, like all they didn't know which was which.

When Jake was four he sat at the old oak table swinging his feet from his chair, his parents smiling lovingly from the other side. His father held out his fist.

"Would you like a present?"

"Yes please Daddy."

His father opened his fist revealing a small yellow disc. It glistened and winked at Jake.

"Thank you Daddy. What is it?"

"It's money Jakey. If you're good we'll give you more each week."

His mother smiled.

"I have a present for you too."

Jake's eyes lit up.

She put a blue pig in front of him. It had a cute nose, big smile and a hole on top.

"What is it Mummy?"

"It's a piggy bank."

"What's that?"

She tapped the pig on the hole.

"It takes care of your money. If you want you can put it in here to keep for later."

Jake eyed the pig cautiously. He dropped the yellow disc into the pig, the pig squealed and its eyes lit up. Jake giggled, clapped his hands.

When Jake was five he sat at the old oak table, toes just touching the ground, his parents smiling lovingly from the other side. His father held his mother's hand.

"Jakey, we have some news."

"Uh huh Daddy."

"Mummy's pregnant, soon you will have a sister."

"Why?"

"We wanted you to have someone to play with."

"Oh. Thank you Mummy."

"We will have to be extra good Jakey, mummy will be tired for a long while. We need to save time to do extra things."

"How?"

"You do things quicker. Like your toys. When you put them away don't play with them, just put them away. That way you save a little bit of time to do other things."

"Like my piggy bank?"

"Yes, like that."

When Jake was nine he sat at the old oak table, hands in his lap, his sister now all of four years old sitting to attention opposite him.

"I have a present for you squirt."

Penny smiled.

Jake put a purple ceramic pig with green flowers in front of her.

"Ooh cute! Thank you Jakey."

"It's a piggy bank. Do you know what it does?"

She shook her head.

"It keeps your pocket money safe for later."

Jenny tickled the pig behind its ears, tried to uncurl its tail.

"You've got gazillions!"

"Yes, but I've been saving longer. Watch this."

Jake took out a silver coin, stuck it in the pig's mouth. Its eyes glowed, the pig grunted and slobbered then swallowed the coin.

Jenny giggled, hands over her mouth.

"Want me to teach you how to save money?"

"Yes please!"

"Later I'll show you how to save time."

When Jake was twelve he sat safely strapped into the Alfa Romeo's race harness. His grandfather wrestled the car around the track once then pulled into the pits.

"I hope you enjoyed it, I'm sorry I haven't more time."

"It's ok gramps, I've had a blast."

"Perhaps a rain check?"

"Sounds like a deal."

"You're used to it?"

Jake laughed.

"Totally. Mum and dad are the worst, but I understand. I'm just saving IOUs."

"With the relations you've got you must have a few lifetimes worth."

When Jake was sixteen his sister sat him down on his bed as she tried to straighten his tie. He fidgeted, all nerves and anxiety.

"Sit still or I'll mess this up!"

"Sorry sis."

She stepped back, regarded her handiwork.

"That's better. You like her, she's really cute isn't she?"

"Sure is."

"Cute ones need more money, I'll get it."

She turned, the bedroom walls covered in shelves, the shelves covered in blue and white ceramic pigs. She reached for the nearest white one.

"No, not that one, the last blue one."

"Sorry."

When Jake was eighteen he sat with his parents on the leather couch, his mother quietly crying, his father holding her hand in a vice-like grip. The specialist sat in the armchair opposite, impassive.

"I'm sorry. We've done all we can, all anyone can."

"How long?" his father whispered, suddenly old, frail.

"Six weeks, two months."

"What will it be like?"

"No pain, just growing weariness until one night she falls asleep then doesn't wake up."

"It's not fair, she's only thirteen."

"I know Mister Yancy, I know. Take her home. There's nothing we can do that you can't."

Jake was five weeks older when he sat down on the edge of her bed. Penny stared at him, propped up on her pillows. The house was quiet, their parents out.

"Well squirt, two weeks left."

"Maybe, maybe a bit less. It's the right time."

"Just what I was thinking."

She looked around her room, walls full of shelves, shelves full of ceramic pigs, some purple, some yellow. At the foot of her bed one white pig sat patiently.

"One of yours and one of mine?"

"That feels right."

Jake picked up a yellow pig with one hand and the white one in his other. He held the pigs above Penny.

"Now?"

"Now."

Jake tapped the pigs together, the porcelain cracking then disappearing. Lime green light cascaded into Penny's open mouth as the hours, days and weeks of promises made to them but never kept infused her, renewed her until her life was no longer measured in days but in decades.

Jenny swung her legs around, springing out of bed to the sound of crunching gravel from the driveway below.

END

AHAB

"TICKET 438 ROOM one." The P.A. floundered under the noise of the packed reception area. Sergeant Pat Blanchfield took the flimsy, pushed through the swing doors into the corridor. Five weeks until I call an end to a thirty year career and the Captain's tied me to the front desk with six inches of bullet proof perspex between me and the crazies. He stepped into the interview room and regarded the man opposite.

Not that there was much to see. Late forties or early fifties, a faint red lesion around his neck, no hidden weapons. He held himself with a resigned, expectant air as if watching for trouble that he knew would find him. Pat put the flimsy to one side, flipped the speaker on.

"So, Mister –"

"Wayne, call me Wayne."

"Ok Wayne, why are you here?"

"I want to report a murder, three murders."

"Whose?"

"Mine."

"You killed three people?"

"No, I'm the victim."

"You don't look particularly dead."

"Of course not, somebody found me in time, each time that bastard sent them."

"Which bastard?"

"The one that keeps killing me."

"Settle down. You say you've been killed three times?"

"No, I mean yes, sort of. I mean three times he's tried to kill me, just last week the latest."

"The red mark?"

"Yeah, hung myself I did, he did."

"So you hung yourself?"

"Yes, he made me, just like the other times."

"So he's made you try to kill yourself three times. It's not quite murder is it?"

"I don't see why not. He's made a ruin out of my entire life and everyone's around me, pushed and pushed but won't let me die, just takes me to the edge and back."

"You have proof, witnesses?"

"No, he's very good, very careful."

"The one you say is doing this, you know him?"

"I put all that into the form —"

"Just humor me. Do you know him?"

"Yes, Roger Paulikas. I had an accident years back ..."

"And?"

"I killed his wife."

Pat sighed, rolled the flimsy into a tube and tapped it on the edge of the desk.

"You don't believe me do you officer?"

"Would you?"

"Of course."

"Don't bullshit me."

Pat unrolled the flimsy. Thirty thousand words. He randomly tapped it.

"You say he crippled your father. Dad's alive?"

"Yes, just."

"What would he say if I talked to him?"

"Nothing, he wouldn't know."

Another tap.

"He broke up your first marriage by seducing your wife and daughter?"

"Well yes, he set it up, sent the men, I know it."

"You saw him?"

"No, but —"

Pat held his hand up, tapped again.

"He caused a defect in the Remington .45 ammunition you tried to commit suicide with, rendering you merely functionally impaired not dead?"

"I know it sounds a bit —"

"No, not a bit but totally. You're either a lunatic or you've got an overactive imagination. You kill a man's wife —"

"It was an accident!"

"You kill his wife and your brain goes into overdrive. Of course he wants you dead, who wouldn't? How long'd you do?"

"Eight inside, four paroled outside."

Pat sighed. He's another nut job, an oxygen thief.

"I don't believe you, but you've made a formal complaint and I've got to follow it up. No matter how asinine it is."

"Thank you."

"Don't. You've had your one shot, waste my time with the same complaint again and you're back inside." Pat stood. "I'll call you if I need you."

The driveway crunched underfoot, uniform pink and black polished quartz pebbles glinting and winking, shadows from poplars lining the pathway dancing in front. The gaps in the trees allowed the merest hint of the grounds beyond, a reminder to the penitent of their place, their real status. The estate had a restrained, aloof presence that acknowledged him while making it patently clear his existence or otherwise was a mere detail.

He'd reached the next to last step on the entry when the double oak doors opened revealing an older couple immaculately dressed in black and white. The man bowed stiffly, the woman curtsied.

"Sergeant Blanchfield, you are expected."

Pat was ushered into a large, sparsely furnished room, huge bay windows framing the immaculate grounds beyond. A cut crystal glass appeared beside him, filled from a matching decanter.

"Drink Sergeant? Sir will be available momentarily."

Pat easily spotted the telltale lumps in the ceiling. He smiled, there was no need to make it obvious except to make it obvious, the sensors worked through most materials. But there was value in letting your guests know they were being watched. He finished his glass.

"Sir will see you now Sergeant."

He was shown into another room, heavily but tastefully decorated, windowless, carpeted. Floor to ceiling shelves along one wall containing thin rectangular blocks of varying colors caught his eye.

"I see my collection has your attention Patrick. A hobby of mine, ancient manuscripts. Perhaps you'd like to hold one?"

"No, thank you, I don't think the Department's insurance runs that high."

"Shame. Well, to business shall we?"

Five suited figures stood silently, motionless behind him.

"My legal team, perhaps not the most sociable of individuals but highly efficient."

"I appreciate your time Mr. Paulikas, I'll make this as brief as possible."

"I understand. From what your Captain said you have no choice. A sad little man by all accounts. You'd forgive my lack of sympathy, he may have paid his debt to society but to me, well, how can it be enough?"

"I understand."

"Now, what do you require to put this matter to rest?"

"One answer and, if you'd be kind enough, some house security tapes."

"To the first of course, the second perhaps. Your question?"

"April fifteenth. Where were you that evening?"

"The fifteenth? From eight in the morning to midnight I was in this room taking care of my … philanthropic interests."

"Your staff, the man and woman at the door, they were here with you?"

"Yes, both were here. You may take statements or talk to them if you wish."

"Thank you. The other thing, the tapes?"

Roger ushered Pat to the door.

"Yes of course you would like those. I'll see that copies are made for you. Is that sufficient?"

"Yes, I believe it is."

Pat finished his first skim of the housetapes. Nothing, just eighteen hours of a man watching a computer, *What good's owning the world if you're chained to a desk all day? At least soon I won't be.* His eyes rested on an old photo pinned to the cubicle divider. Pat touched his fingers to his lips, his fingers to the photo. *I wonder what it would be like if —"*

The Captain poked her head round the corner.

"Blanchfield, how you going with Paulikas?"

"Slowly. He's complained?"

"Wouldn't be the first time for you but no, he's good. Just let me know when you've closed it."

"Yeah, will do."

Pat spun the housetapes again. All ordinary and boring, he was about to wipe them when something caught his eye. As Paulikas sat in his chair his left arm shimmered, the thumb on his left hand winking in and out. The time coding showed no tampering, no splicing. Pat pulled on the headset, jacked into the VR system.

He popped up inside the rendering of the room and moved to one side of Paulikas. As Paulikas' thumb flickered a dark patch on the back of his shirt appeared. He could see the computer on the desk clearly, showing a shop interior and a man climbing a ladder in front of a wall of small boxes. The man pulled a small red box out of the wall of yellow-blue ones. The hairs on the back of Pat's neck stood up. The box in his hand bore the logo 'Remington. RimFire ScatterShot .45'.

The housetapes gave him more, Paulikas' computer showing Wayne entering the shop, the man handing the box to him. Paulikas had turned the screen on as Wayne entered, turned it off as Wayne left.

Pat dismissed the thumb and the shirt from his mind, concentrating on the ammunition. He refilled his coffee, settled back and interrogated the AI.

After an hour Pat was none the wiser. There was nothing linking Paulikas to the shop. Yet the housetapes remained a clear reminder there must be some link. Pat shook his head. *What if it's Remington,* what if it's the ammunition? He got back to work with the AI.

— How many weapons use this type of ammunition?

— Four.

— How many weapons are in circulation?

— Three hundred fifty seven thousand.

— How many of the type used by the complainant?

— Twenty eight.

— Which if any of the ammunition components could cause the complainant's weapon to fail but not any others?

— One.

— Describe component and failure.

— Percussion cap cover is one one-thousandth too thick to properly discharge resulting in greatly retarded projectile muzzle velocity.

— What would be the result of using the complainant's weapon and the identified ammunition to attempt suicide?

— Ninety-five percent chance moderate to severe, five percent chance minor, non-life threatening injuries.

— Is the percussion cap cover manufactured by Remington?

— No. Manufactured by IamonCorp.

— Has or does Paulikas or known associates have any association with IamonCorp?

— Paulikas Trust 298 gained controlling interest of IamonCorp in 1973. IamonCorp outsourced R&D and CAD/CAM functions to Aartech in 2013. Aartech is a fully owned subsidiary of Paulikas Trust 476.

— When did manufacture of percussion caps for this type of ammunition commence?

— 2028

Well over one hundred years ago. It was impossible for it to mean what Wayne had claimed yet there it was, everything except Paulikas himself writing the dimensions, feeding it to the CAD/CAM. It has to be coincidence, just random events glued together the wrong way in Wayne's mind. Pat flipped through the flimsy looking for one more claim to check. The crippled father. That ought to do it.

Pat waited until the following Monday. A week sitting, mulling it all over had left him more uncertain, more confused. He touched his fingers to his lips, fingers to the photo, then opened a comms link.

"Captain, got a minute?"

"What?"

"The Paulikas complaint. I've just NFA'd it. I was going to go out, let Mr. Paulikas know."

"Fine."

The butler was waiting, ushering Pat directly into Mr. Paulikas' presence. This time they were alone.

"So Patrick, what can I do for you?"

"I've come to let you know I've rejected the complaint."

"I appreciate it but you could have just called. You have something else on your mind?"

"Well, not so much but … do you mind if I try out your desk for a minute or two?"

"Why?"

"I've never owned one, never got this close to a real wooden desk. I'm retiring soon and I won't get the chance again."

"Why not? Go on, indulge yourself."

Pat went across, sat down slowly and spread his arms out wide, fingertips falling well short of the edges. He looked up, grinning like a young schoolboy.

"That feels amazing."

"You wouldn't believe the number of people who've wanted to sit where you are, most of them hoping it was over my dead body."

Pat sat back, head firmly against the headrest, arms along the sides of the chair.

"I suppose none of us go through life without making a few enemies."

"If you live properly."

Pat surreptitiously felt for buttons, levers, indents with his hands. There were none. He stood.

"I'd better give it back before I get used to it."

"Believe me Patrick, you never would. I haven't."

"Wealth, influence, respect? It's not too hard imagining being very comfortable indeed."

"Perhaps, but to get here you need to play the tough man, be hard hearted and hard minded. It doesn't stop, it gets worse and more serious once you have something to protect."

"But the compensations —"

"Oh yes, undoubtedly. When I started I had to save to buy lunch, now if I'm hungry I just buy the restaurant. But in the end we are only men, our appetites the same, just the scale that varies. Tell me Patrick, why didn't you remarry after Stefania died?"

"I don't know, I've never really thought about it."

"Twelve years is a long time celibate."

"Celibate? Oh no, hardly. It's just … I don't know, commitment I guess. No one could ever take her place so I never tried."

"Precisely."

"And you Mr. —"

"Please, Roger will do."

"Roger, what about you?"

"The same. You see, underneath we are closer than you think. So Patrick, back to business. The matter is closed?"

"Yes, officially."

"Meaning to you it's not."

"A few strange things bother me."

"Such as?"

Pat described what he had found, the thumb, the shimmer, the ammunition, the father's accident. Through it all Roger sat silent, impassive.

"You caught me off guard the other day with your request for the housetapes."

"As I said, officially it's over. Unofficially I don't want mysteries to dog me through retirement."

"Do you like mind games Patrick?"

"I like them fine."

"Tell me. If you could would you stop Stefania getting on that flight?"

"Of course."

"And if you couldn't, if she was on it no matter what?"

"I'd stop the plane, close the airport."

"If you couldn't do that?"

"I don't know … kidnap the pilot or sabotage the jet, anything to stop it."

"That's how I felt with Agnes. What do you know about history?"

"Not much, I never studied it."

"Nearly everyone believes the past is set in stone, fixed and unchanging except for the myths and lies we drape around it. I met a brilliant woman once who claimed it wasn't."

"What did she think?"

"She said time was a river, and we simply swimmers in it. The river may have to go east to west but it doesn't care if it goes a little north or south as long as it reaches the ocean."

"I don't get it."

"Neither did I at first. She meant that the big stuff, the key events and people were fixed, had to happen, but the rest could change and no one would know or care."

"It's a nice theory but what's the use?"

"Let's say you go back to old America. You walk into a bar and you deliberately knock a man's drink over. You buy him another one, walk out, come back. Tell me, what's history say about it?"

"Well, I guess it just sees me spill his drink."

"But you'd have to see it not being spilt to spill it."

"I guess, but isn't that a problem?"

"That's what I thought. But this is the thing. She said everything that could happen, all the changes ever made to the past, had already happened. All you had to do was work out where you fit in, what you did, and do it. So if you were going to go back in time, spill the guy's drink, it's always been that way, time is just waiting for you to see it and do what you were always going to do."

"All well and good but it's still just a game."

"Perhaps, but indulge me a little further. What's the statute of limitations for murder?"

"The longest I know of is Ontario, thirty years I think, although there's a rumor New Mexico's going to push for fifty."

"Fine, fifty years. Pretend you go back a hundred years, you kill someone at random. Just put a bullet through her head in broad daylight, let them take your photo ID then come back. Can we prosecute you now for her murder?"

"I don't think so. I'm not sure, I mean, a hundred years ago but it's now ... sort of."

"Exactly. You couldn't, I couldn't, no one could. If anyone tried any half decent lawyer would tie any judge or jury into knots."

"You might be right."

"I know I am, or at least my legal team says so."

Roger got up, sat behind his desk.

"No more games Patrick. This woman, when she told me this, when I met her, Agnes had been gone two years. She, or rather what she said, became my sole consuming passion for five years. I threw everything I had, all my resources, everything at her disposal."

Pat finished his drink slowly, set the glass down.

"Why didn't you simply stop him?"

"I tried, believe me I tried everything. But it couldn't be done, it wasn't possible. Every single thing I did failed and failed spectacularly. Bullets missed, poisons didn't work, roadblocks opened up. I couldn't change where Agnes was, couldn't stop her, slow her down. History needed her dead, demanded her death then and there. And each time I tried and failed it killed me a little more."

"How many times did you try?"

"More than a thousand."

"And Agnes was that important to the world?"

"No! That's the damned thing, it's not her but ... but something else, and I had to see it again and again and again until I found out, watching her, powerless. I was not a vindictive man Patrick, a hard business man but never vindictive, but it changed me. If I couldn't get Agnes back I was going to make him suffer, suffer for his entire life, from birth to death and beyond if I could."

"So everything Wayne said —"

"Oh yes, and more, so much more. It's so easy, so simple. Buy a company, change a specification, shift a timetable, seduce, bribe or corrupt the right people. Go back as far as you need, make the tiniest change that ten, fifty, two hundred years later impacts one individual and one alone. Go as far forward as you want and drag the tech back, make the impossible possible. All I had to do was sit here, work it out, watch what I had already done and then just go back and do it."

"But there's no time machine. Your chair's —"

"Irrelevant. What do you think, it's as big as the old mainframes? It's tiny, so tiny." He tapped his forehead. "It's in here, a microscopic switch, that's all. When she told me I thought it was a lie, my god how wrong I was."

"But the chair, the twitch of your thumb?"

"I can't go back and simply pop out of thin air just anywhere. I bought this estate four hundred years ago, this chair immobile in this one spot, this room locked and secured by the best of the future's technology the entire time. My thumb? You try coming back and sitting in exactly the same pose after months."

"How long has this been going on?"

"Ten years, but I've lived thirty or more in them."

"Has it been worth it?"

"Are you kidding? Yes, everything, every second wrecking every part of his life, hopes and dreams from the start through to when he dies a shattered, abject failure. His father, his sister, his jobs, his career, children, friends, money, loves it's all been worth it, every second and every cent to destroy it all from his name onwards."

"His name?"

"Of course, what sort of idiot would call their son Wayne? Wayne Anka? Mr. W. Anka? He's tried a hundred times to change it and will try a hundred more but he will never succeed."

"Revenge destroys you, it's never worth it."

"Oh? Put yourself in my shoes. Would you have done anything else?"

Pat stared at the empty glass. It was useless, impossible to be another person, feel the world and emotions as they did. A sliver, the slightest crack of insight opened to him and there he was, Roger being there over and over and over watching the only love in his life torn away and he impotent to stop it, an unwilling voyeur tortured until all-consuming anguish and hatred erupted. Suddenly it was Stefania and not Agnes being wrenched away and Pat was changing the safety guard on the drill press that would take a man's arm off, baiting the merchant bankers into strip mining a family's life savings,

159

encouraging Lothario to deflower a boy's first love before he had the guts to try. Pat found himself relishing it, chafing at the bit to hit harder, gouge deeper, crush the very spirit out of Wayne and everything associated with him completely, deliberately, methodically. Pat slumped, looked up with eyes devoid of pity but filled with understanding at the empty man opposite. He stood.

"Goodbye Roger. I'm truly sorry."

Roger watched as Pat let himself out. It wasn't right, none of it was right and if he had the power he'd change it but, perhaps mercifully, he didn't. If she had died a minute earlier, a minute later then it would have been possible. But the child was there, the child that would become the man that long after Roger and Pat were dust would save the world. And my Agnes, my beautiful Agnes' death the sole catalyst for his passion. To the boy who would become the man a nameless face; to the world that would survive because of him unknown.

He cried as only an old man can cry, tortured as only he could ever be. If I cannot for myself then maybe for another, and they'll never know. He leant back, eyes closed for a few seconds, flickered out and back.

Pat headed home. He'd lost any desire to go back to the office, face the troubles and issues knowing there was a way to change what couldn't be changed as long as it was already changed. Maybe the Captain would let him burn some sick leave, hopefully four weeks' worth until he retired.

Retired. He smiled, glanced at the photo on the dash, touched his fingers to his lips, fingers to the photo. She was waiting at home as always, and maybe now he could give her the attention she deserved. Stefania, my Stefania, the world would mean nothing without you.

END

OUT OF AFRICA

HE CAME INTO the world when she was thirteen, alone and friendless, the midwife hurriedly turning her back on the mud walled hut. She held him scared and nervous as the last light filtered through the open plains of the delta, serenaded by the hyena's call and thrashing legs through grass. She thought his face beautiful, handsome.

"You are loved Tsabo."

He was four when she found him naked and silent on the ground, Milky Way a warming blanket to her spirit in the still autumn night. She lay next to him staring as if the heavens could bring back her people, his father, her lover. What more to life than this, a strange child, a strange universe, a riddle without clues?

"You know they will not let me be mother."

"I have waited for your first words. These were not my hope."

"They are what they are. They are for you alone."

"We still have time?"

"We still have time."

When he was seven they returned him as fast as he was taken. She read fear on their faces.

"There is nothing for us to do Anna, nothing to teach."

"Is not my son smart?"

"We have nothing to give he does not have. He is our equal and more."

Tsabo sat silent cross-legged on the dirt, the baked earth's dust a thousand lost dreams rising, swirling.

"Then what is to become of him?"

"We have filled the papers, he has passed the school. As the lower, the higher. What more is up to him."

Tsabo stirred.

"Do not concern yourself for my sake. The blind may only teach the blind."

He was ten when he came to her restless and troubled. They sat as mother and son, adult and child, pupil and teacher.

"I must leave this place."

"Why?"

"There is more to this world than the limit of your eyes."

"May I come?"

"If you wish."

When he was twelve the reek of butter and goat milk clung to her, sandalwood ash floating down to the stones on which she lay. Five days and five nights he sat unmoving as the mandala was made and unmade, chants sung and unsung.

"... eternal unbound, the shell an illusion the dream reality." Lumbum whispered to her.

"To what end? If the I dissolves then the I will fight."

"As it must, yet the I must conquer the I, a sacrifice to itself, an eternal stream of consciousness, rebirth and redeath."

Tsabo stood.

"If you look inside you do not see without. If you look outside you do not see within. To see everything you must not look at all."

When he was twenty they bought him back as they had taken him. Unforced, unshackled, silent. They stood respectfully, persecutors and victim, captors and prisoner, weakness and power.

"We are deafened by his silence. We are weakened by his submission."

"What have you done to my son in this year you have stolen from me?"

"Nothing he did not allow."

"Which is?"

"Everything mother. Strength flows only from weakness, dominion from servitude."

They scorned him when he was thirty, denying him power and authority he never sought. For fear of the world they embraced him, for love of themselves they rejected him; their self-loathing sent him away. They turned their faces rich from poor, powerful from weak, disease from cure.

"You are not for us so you must be against."

"You say nothing against us so your heart must condemn."

"The people hear you so your words must be lies."

Tsabo wept.

"A mirror held to the world sees the truth; the world sees only the light it chooses to cast."

He was thirty three when they came for him in the evening desert coolness. The old one of full beard and missing eye; the youthful one with blue skin and seven snakes; the one of saffron and buttered skin; the one with pierced hands. She searched their eyes as they searched her heart.

"What is it you will make of him?"

"Nothing he has not made of himself."

"Why do I see my son in your eyes?"

"The reason we see him in all, the circle is complete. The beginning is as false as the end. The illusion of time itself an illusion, the stream a point, the many the one."

The light burned from five as one. As the light increased the stars faded to impenetrable eternal dark.

"Come to the light mother."

END

IN WHOSE NAME

SHE IS TERRIFIED, wide eyes fixed on me, breath shallow, sweat across her brow. I lean closer, make sure she is secure. There are none to interfere or overhear in the crowded square, everyone keeping their distance perhaps out of respect, certainly out of fear. I steady myself.

"You understand why, what I have told you?"

She nods, cracked teeth biting her lower lip.

"When it catches do not fight the fire, it will only prolong the pain. When I nod embrace it, lean into it and breathe deeply, it will hasten your journey."

I step away leaving her isolated atop the pyre of wood, a solitary figure surrounded by empty gray flagstones, flagstones in turn encircled by the village in its entirety. It is necessary and right they should see, be reminded it is their very souls at risk and the lengths the church will go to protect them.

Miguelito hands me the torch, a pitch-dipped flaming rag sputtering and spitting in the still air. I walk the short distance to the pyre and place the torch down.

I lock my eyes to hers as the flames take hold and her screams rise, pitched wailings of agony as her legs start to be consumed, her clothes filthy rags smoking then bursting alight. Gasps and muted prayers rise around me, the click of beads as Father Ignacio races through the Hail Marys. Her eyes remain fixed and as the flames reach her waist I nod. She bends forwards, soundlessly mouthing as she breaths the fire deeply, strongly, slumping forwards unmoving against her bonds.

The flames roar higher, the rising wind carrying smoke and the scent of burning flesh over me. Neither the sickly sweet smell nor the sounds of vomiting and abhorrence are unfamiliar. I will stay until her very bones are ash as will everyone around me lest they incur my displeasure, be seen not to understand and accept the discipline of the church. The smoke starts to sting, permeate my clothes but my gaze remains, countenance set, hands steady. A shower of sparks flare upwards as she settles into the pyre, bonds breaking, charred smoldering stumps that once were arms flailing outwards in embrace macabre. Stifled cries from my left join muted prayer from the right.

It is only hours later with the pyre reduced to a low mound of embers that I shift my gaze slowly and deliberately across everyone gathered in the square. None had dared leave. Fear, obedience, belief meet me. For her family hatred and sorrow salt the wounds, a wasteful and unfeeling god allowing disease to take four children before they were six and one to heresy when not yet thirteen.

Beads still clicking through his fingers, Ignacio's pasty white face stares through unseeing eyes. He has no desire to be here but it is his duty. A small cough gains his attention.

"You must tend your flock."

Ignacio stares at me, stumbling to find thought or word in response. It is hardest the first time, he's probably married her parents, baptized the child, watched her grow.

"Remember Ignacio, remember why and rejoice. Her confession the other day, her walk back from heresy."

"Yes Brother Anteo," unconvinced, uncertain "she gains eternal life through the purifying fire." He smiles wanly. "Saved from heresy, a lesson, a teaching in truth to us all."

I squeeze Ignacio's shoulder then move past him, Miguelito in tow, towards my room. A lesson perhaps, a waste certainly.

I slip my sandals off, stretch my tired legs as Miguelito prepares the salve. The days and miles are hard on old feet and the work endless, the welcomes unfailingly forced. Here perhaps a little warmer, a touch more open, Ignacio not having the company of an inquisitor before. The invitation to sup remained. I tapped

Miguelito's head, mouthed the words slowly.

"Do you wish to accept Father Ignacio's hospitality again?"

Miguelito smiled, shook his head. A near-deaf mute was the perfect choice of attendant but it created its own peculiar worries. It was also no fun for Miguelito. What business could a young boy have in the company of two old men?

"Then go, return to me in the morning. Do I have to remind you not to bring shame on this office? I have not forgotten, nor has the girl's parents."

Miguelito shook his head, clasping his hands in promise. His eyes betrayed the memory, youthful lusts still written large. I sighed, waved him away.

Ignacio was shaken but welcoming, the meal simple and plentiful, eaten in silence as the order required. We sat alone at table, cups of wine in hand as the evening darkness ate into the solitary candle's glow.

"The other, your business will be concluded soon?"

"Of course. One day, perhaps two, no more."

"Then?"

"Wherever I am led."

"You have performed this … duty for a while?"

"Four years, perhaps longer, I keep no account."

"The calling must be strong, it is not a thing I could do."

"You would were you asked. But yes, the calling was clear."

It could not have been clearer, simpler, more unsettling. Alone in my cell fasting and praying for fourteen days it had happened on the last evening. Pitch black as I extinguished the candle one second, an explosion of light the next, it stood within arm's reach towering in front of me clad in shimmering silver-white, burning halo, wings touching either wall. All my faculties deserted me, I stood unmoving, uncomprehending in its presence. 'You are called,' it spoke in a hundred voices, lips unmoving 'and you will do your work diligently as unto the most high.' All I could do was shake, mumble incoherently. It placed a crucifix and a book on the edge of my cot. It stepped closer, close enough for me to feel the cold surrounding it, the iciness of the fire. 'You will tell no one born of woman what you find, of the relics I have given you.' It grabbed me, held me, two hands to my head, two hands to my sides, eyes fixing me, mesmerizing me. 'You will invoke the most extreme penalty on the heretic. It is not enough they recant, they must be removed.' It opened the book. 'Seek me while holding this and I will send you,' then pointed to the crucifix 'and invoke this to remove the stain of heresy from both heretic and earth.' With that I was released and my cell returned to its former dark, empty state.

"The say the Holy Father takes a care for each inquisitor sent."

"That is true, each of us is sent by him."

That night, alone with the relics, I was left to worry. I could not simply walk out claiming visitation; I would suffer the same fate as any madman doing so. And with my vows taken, my life's path set, I was not free to change vocation. How small my faith was, for on the morrow the Abbott handed me the warrant from the Holy Father. I opened it to reveal the hand of Gregory IX, tiny droplets of ink across the page witnessing a hasty, uncertain scrawl. I was to have no master above me save himself and God, and I was to be sole judge and agent, alone responsible for sentence and execution.

Ignacio sighed, leant back into the shadows.

"He expects us to lead them in faith by example, but an unruly flock at times needs a firm hand."

"And that is my calling."

Yet even from the start my faith was challenged. As I kneeled in prayer that night in my cell worrying uselessly about the morning I saw the water where my visitor stood. What need of water does an angel have I asked. Another mystery awaited for, as I touched the wet stone it brought back a scrap of fabric layered, white upon silver upon black upon white and fine, thinner than silk and smoother than polished metal. What angel garbed themselves in cloth? I have kept that scrap with me all these years, one scrap of doubt tucked away in my cassock while other scraps gathered in my mind.

Ignacio stood.

"The day has been long. It has drained me I fear. I pray I will have the strength to accept it, to grow accustomed to it as you have. I bid you good night."

I watched him leave. I would never grow accustomed to it, don the garb of indifference or rejoicing other inquisitors wore. No matter Miguelito's efforts my clothes always bore that sickly sweet smell, the hearth contained their eyes, my joy in the bonfire's warmth replaced by the horror of the pyre. Nor was there solace in the sacraments now as hollow cymbals to me, or in the dark as my mind changed sleep to a seldom seen friend.

The guards at the door regarded me differently this morning. Respect and curiosity was replaced by fear and submission. It was one thing to be told a man had power over body and soul in this world and the next, another thing entirely to see it exercised. Miguelito and I passed inside knowing the door was closed and we would remain undisturbed. Once the village's butchering room, a new butcher now simply occupied it. I sat in the sole chair, relics cradled in the bag on my lap. Miguelito poured a ladle of water over the head of the naked man chained to the far wall.

He raised his head, scarlet-cream threads of the week's encouragement adorning his filth encrusted skin. A piteous human seeking mercy I could not give. When I came here he truly had no concept of his error, my purpose, his future. The simplest of a village of simpletons, his very innocence sealed his fate, one a smarter man would have closed his mouth and mind to avoid.

"Let us continue Sebastian. Miguelito, tend the fire."

The fire spurted, black irons starting their transformation to dull red.

"I will say what you want, as you want it your holiness."

"Yes, you will, but it is not what matters. This is to save your soul, prepare you for God. Would you want to be before him unworthily, a liar in your heart?"

"No."

"Nor would I. All this is to your benefit, your salvation. Tell me of the things you saw."

"I saw nothing, I swear, nothing."

I nodded to Miguelito. Miguelito was careful and precise, the scream rent from Sebastian short, piercing. A wisp of smoke arose from his little toe.

"Truth Sebastian, truth. What you saw and what you thought are different. Again, tell me what you saw."

"Angels, two angels in a —"

Another caress from Miguelito halted him.

"Again, what did you see?"

"Men?"

"Good. Tell me again, what did you see?"

I signaled Miguelito.

"Men, I saw men, men, two men," a screaming wail as the iron passed the underside of his foot.

"Good. Men. Do not lie before me or before God. Now, remind me of that which we talked of yesterday. Describe the men to me."

"They were tall."

"Good. More."

"They were bright, shiny."

"And?"

"And?"

"Yes, and."

"They had, they had wings?"

I smiled, hopefully reassuringly.

"Very good. You see, nothing to fear from the truth. Now, again, what were they doing?"

"Looking down."

"At what?"

"An animal, a dead animal."

"Anything else?"

"They took pieces of it."

"And?"

"I don't know, they just took pieces and left."

"How did they leave?"

"They just went, they were there and then they were not."

I walked over, close enough to smell his rotting teeth. I placed one hand on his cheek now wet with tears.

"Do you see? Your memory, the truth is there. You are nearly ready."

I stepped back, motioned Miguelito to the far side of the room.

"Now tell me, who were these men?"

"I don't know."

I lifted a white hot iron to his face.

"No your holiness, please, they were angels."

I thrust the iron into a bucket of water, withdrawing it hissing and smoking.

"Please, I don't know. Angels, I don't know, please."

I stepped towards him, iron held out still smoking, glowing dark crimson. He struggled against the chains, eyes wide. It was still a puzzle to me how the smoking yet cooler iron placed more fear into their hearts than when white hot.

"I don't know, they were who you want them —"

I lifted his member carefully with the tip of the iron, gliding the iron quickly but carefully back to the sack, sliding it down slowly before I returned iron to fire. I let him scream himself hoarse to exhaustion, resuming my seat to consider him. Once the sobbing subsided I continued.

"Sebastian, you disappoint me, you disappoint the Holy Father. Who knows your heart best Sebastian?"

"God?"

"And does not the Holy Father speak with God?"

"Yes."

"And does the Holy Father speak to me?"

"Yes, he does, you told me."

"As God knows your heart, so must the Holy Father know your heart. So do I know your heart?"

"Yes, yes."

"Are you smarter than God, smarter than I Sebastian?"

"No, no your holiness."

"So who knows your heart better Sebastian, you or I?"

"You do."

"The men, your heart knows what they were even if your mind is deceived. They were daemons Sebastian, that is the truth."

Miguelito returned to the fire, stoking the bellows.

"It says in God's book that the devil himself treads the earth as an angel of light to devour the simple, the unwary. You are a simple man Sebastian, easy prey for the evil one."

The shaking returned, his voice staccato cartwheels over cobblestones.

"Yes your holiness."

"It is for you the church exists, to save your eternal soul. The devil ensnared you Sebastian, and I am here to set you free. Our bodies and our minds are but traps, traps for the devil to use."

I stood, walked within arm's reach of him. Miguelito drew near, two irons in hand.

"You were deceived, your mind clouded from the truth. Who were the men Sebastian?"

"They, they were daemons."

"You must believe, not simply hope. Who were they?"

"Daemons."

"You must believe, Sebastian, believe. Who were they?"

"Daemons, devils both."

Miguelito danced the irons across his back.

"Before God himself," I screamed, my spittle showering his face "who were they?"

"Daemons!" he screamed back, and we stood there, I screaming the question, he screaming the answer accompanied by the hiss of irons and writhing feet squelching in excrement as he tried in vain to break his chains.

I signaled Miguelito to cease; Sebastian hung limp.

"Daemons, daemons all." he spat through gasps and whimpers. "I am deceived, damned for eternity."

I lifted his face to mine.

"You know the truth of it now, how easily you were snared."

He nodded, sweat and drool cascading over my fingers, onto my cassock. I leant forwards, kissed him on the forehead.

"You are no longer deceived, you will not be damned. You are ready to face God, prepared for Him. I can release you from the pain and deceptions, save your soul. Do you want me to?"

He nodded vigorously, eyes now wet with hope.

"Tomorrow the fire will purge your body, send your soul to God, saved for all eternity. Do you want this?"

"Please, yes please your holiness, yes."

I reached behind me into the bag and pulled the crucifix out, holding it to his face. The effect was immediate, his breathing slowing, his eyes fixed on the Christ as it glowed opalescent, tiny shards of colored light dancing across Sebastian's nose.

"I envy you. Tomorrow through a brief veil of pain you shall see God."

I stood there until the crucifix returned to wood and stepped out, Miguelito in tow. The guards sprang upright, but not quickly enough to disguise their eavesdropping. I turned to Miguelito.

"Get some water and clean him, give him to eat and drink. Do not tarry as we have more work."

I turned to the guards.

"Keep a mind to your work and my words. There is room in the fire for more than this one."

I walked through the square, back to my room closing the door after me. I placed the bag on the cot, crossed to the small enclosed courtyard beyond. I sank to my knees shaking under the olive tree, heaving out my breakfast and the previous evening's meal until winded and emptied. I tipped on my side, cold shivers rippling along my body, hands pulling my knees tight to my chest. Waste, waste, only waste.

By the time Ignacio and Miguelito returned I was composed, cleaned, the afternoon sun a bloated orb wallowing towards the horizon.

"Is it wise to go there?"

"Miguelito and I will be fine."

"You do not wish me to accompany you?"

"No. Stay and prepare for tomorrow."

Ignacio watched on uncertainly as Miguelito and I left, walked out of the village and disappeared over a small rise.

We walked a little way then I rested, taking the book from my bag. Of itself it was an object of beauty, small, leather bound, the handwritten parchment precise, impossibly symmetrical and without error. It must have taken months for someone to copy it out, to illustrate it in such detail. I opened it at the twenty-third psalm and did as I had been told, placing my finger on the page and translating the Latin to the vulgate in my mind.

"The Lord is my shepherd I shall not want."

I had no sooner finished than the vision came to me, the small clearing, copse, low rocky outcrop in the middle. Half an hour's walk, to the left, past the brook. I stood, strode confidently away.

Reality again matched imagining. I left Miguelito at the edge of the clearing, making my way to the rocks. Just as Sebastian had described, an animal lay spread eagled across one boulder in perfect symmetry, untouched by scavengers. It was at least one week dead yet had no signs of decay. I pressed my finger against the cold flesh which bounced back against my touch. The skull and backbone had been cleft in two, the cut a precise and clean stroke betraying an unmatched ease and effortlessness. Here and there holes had been cut, perfect circles down through the flesh, organs and bone, some to the rock itself. I placed my finger in one hole, moved it around and drew it out bloodied, dripping.

I shook my head, it was the same as I had seen on occasion over the years, animal, beast or human but always the same, laid out precisely even lovingly, life erased and replaced by mystery. At my first three years ago I had wondered what satanic ritual drove such things; then later at what purpose taking the same pieces from such diverse examples could be; to now a sickening questioning over the wasteful repetitiveness of it all.

I removed the crucifix from my bag, held it glowing bright green above the animal. I paced my way slowly to Miguelito, stopping in front of him as the crucifix resumed its wooden pallor. He looked at me expectantly, I pointing to the spot just in front of him.

I separated Christ from the cross and handed Him across.

"Sit, wait."

I returned to the animal, placed the cross upon it, and returned to sit next to Miguelito. He handed me the Christ quickly, smiling and fidgeting in anticipation. He always looked forwards to this as, I would admit, did I.

"Miguelito remember, this is holy work and should be done somberly. This time please, no clapping."

I grasped one arm of the Christ in each hand, placed my lips against the back of His head and turned Him towards the animal. A beam of light sprung between Christ and cross, a swirling rainbow of color expanding to a dome encompassing the animal and the clearing. It stayed there, a dancing wall of color and sparks occasionally lit by flashes of lightning from within until a minute or so later it receded rapidly to the cross, extinguishing itself with a flash and barely audible pop.

I turned to see Miguelito leaning forwards, a child's smile of delight on his face. He saw me just in time to stop his hands meeting in midair.

"Yes, that was colorful but still no reason for that. Stay here while I get the cross."

I stood, walked to the rock. The grass crunched under foot, the air smelling as it does after a storm. The cross had returned to wood and lay quietly atop the rotting remains of the animal, slack skin enveloping bones wrapped in putrefied flesh. I lifted the cross and saw a small object under the animal's hide. I tugged at it, revealing it to be a thick silver disc as broad as my palm, cold and smooth. It began to vibrate, sending tingles down my fingers. I had seen this once before. I dropped it where I found it, hurried back to Miguelito while jamming the Christ back on the cross.

"Go now back to the village. I will join you shortly."

He pointed to the sun now resting on the horizon.

"No, I will be safe. You must go, go now."

He shook his head again. I grabbed his shoulders.

"Miguelito. They are coming back, the angels of God or the daemons, I know not which. Do you want to burn at the stake?

He paled visibly, concern on his face.

"I will be protected by the relics but you are vulnerable. Run back to the village and wait. Worry yourself not about me."

Without further encouragement he turned and fled. I sat low against a tree, partly obscured by the grasses.

I didn't have long to wait, the sun barely replaced by the moon when the clearing was transformed from soft silver to glaring blue white light. Four figures appeared in silver white clothing, burning halos around their heads. But none bore wings, and the four were of different statures. Here now these perfect beings were before me but each was different. How could that be? And no wings, so how could they travel? Small doubts piled on small doubts gathered over the years.

They circled around the rocks, one taking a stick from its back and waving it, one cupping a hand to its ear chanting silent incantations to the sky. One picked up the disc and placed it within its vestments. Another approached it, spoke in earnest, then pointed in my general direction. The other nodded, the first one moving towards me in haste. I pushed myself deeper into the grass, hand in bag clutching the relics.

It stopped perhaps twenty paces to my left, leaning with one arm against a tree. I started reciting the psalms in my mind, my fingers driving between the covers of the book. The figure shifted slightly, its free hand moving to its waist then, with a sigh a stream of liquid passed between it and the tree, spattering droplets clear to me. It took a second for my mind to understand it. It was relieving itself? An angel? A daemon? Only flesh and blood needed to but if that were so —

My thoughts were erased by the vision in my head. My hand, my fingers in the book had sought out the well-worn page and now the vision of the clearing overlay my view of it. Instantly the four figures turned to look, walked unerringly to me until I was surrounded. I shook uncontrollably, my bowels loosed themselves, and I waited for judgment.

One raised an arm holding a short gray rod, the one beside it grasping it with one hand, waving the other three vigorously. They seemed to argue, pointing at me, the sky, each other until one looked a little closer at me, the spreading stain on my cassock, and drew the others' attention. They stood briefly in silence then started to laugh, deep throated noises. Three of them disappeared, leaving me alone with the tall one. It placed a finger behind one ear. The hundred voices returned from lips unmoving.

"You. Again. Was not the last time enough?"

"It was late, an accident."

"You should have left with your boy."

"I was curious."

"You should not be. Do you forget your instructions?"

"No."

The hundred voices were now ten thousand, crashing through

my skull.

"Then stay to those and no more! Do you doubt that we can inflict worse upon you than the flames do to those you deliver?"

"I do not doubt."

It bent down, placed an ice cold finger under my chin and lifted my face.

"Oh but you do Anteo, you do. Simple, simple man, your mind is an open page to me. You doubt everything since our first time but you do not have the words to say how. And I will not give them."

It stood, stepped back

"Take a care with your work. Do not disappoint us again." with which it disappeared, and I into the night.

Sebastian was terrified, wide eyes fixed on me, breath shallow. Beneath the fear the eyes showed faith, trust, hope, fixed on what lay hours away not within the hour. I leant closer, making sure he was secured to the pole. There was none to interfere or overhear in the crowded square, everyone keeping their distance. I steadied myself.

"When it catches do not fight the fire, it will only prolong the pain. When I nod embrace it, lean into it and breathe deeply, it will hasten your journey."

"Thank you your holiness, thank you for helping me to see the truth."

I locked my eyes to his, and as the flames danced around his waist I nodded.

Truth. What is that? There is no truth in this, just lies as there were for the others.

Yet still I continue.

END

PICTURES OF YOU

DEATH ALWAYS SMELLS the same. Yuichi adjusted her blue plastic overalls then picked her way between fast food containers, betting slips and soiled laundry littering the floor to pull back the curtains and let in the Osaka morning. Another day, another cleanup, another invisible death. The sofa carried the indentations, dark stained upholstery to one end and a few strands of short black hair on the other.

Takeshi came through the front door, cleaning cart in tow.

"Six months this one. They said they had trouble separating flesh from vinyl. Wouldn't have known except for the cats."

Takeshi wasn't cruel; it was the necessary armor for the job. Yuichi had to treat each one as a thing, forget the person who had lived and suffered and died alone. There was only enough room to mourn one and that space was filled.

The cleaning wasn't difficult. The bodies were all desiccated flesh, fluids drained into furniture or floor to be discarded beyond repair. The rest just stubborn stains, piles of ingrained filth, remnants of grating lives abandoned to isolation in a world of cheek to jowl connection.

The boxing's confronting, to get the meager assortment of things sorted and tagged. Old photographs, smiling faces and bright eyed children staring out watching a stranger remove the last earthly trace of an unknown other. Yuichi's armor had thickened, nothing moved her, all of it intellectual curiosity as she traded time for the means to survive.

Just past midday they stood at the doorway looking past two small sealed cartons to a clean, freshly aired room. Seventy-five years walking this earth and all that remains would fit under my sink. Takeshi placed two orange garbage bags on the cart. Yuichi bowed deeply, stepped backwards and closed the door.

"You always do that. They do not see or care."

"Once someone did. Forgetting is impolite."

"Whatever. Lunch then see what's next?"

Her boss like all bosses was tight fisted. The cheap soba was in character, keeping her hand out of his pocket. Yuichi slurped away steadily.

Takeshi reached for a pen.

"They have a small one for tomorrow but my daughter has an appointment. You will be able to manage by yourself."

It was no request. It never was.

"Of course."

He scrawled hurriedly on a napkin.

"I will leave the cart inside the door tonight. This is the address and entry code. I will meet you there at six pm tomorrow."

It could not be called an apartment. Shared bathroom and kitchen, what was left barely six paces across. She pushed past the cart to pull up the blind, the wall of concrete and glass opposite blocking all but the faintest reflection of a smog tinted day.

It's a mistake, perhaps Takeshi has already done the work. No, a check of the address said it was the right place, the folded orange bags and stacked empty boxes awaiting her attention. The room was nearly bare. Just the stale scent of decay blanketing a wooden chair and table, a framed photograph, a small pile of soiled clothes. An hour's work, maybe less. Perhaps Takeshi was softening, handing over easier jobs.

An elderly woman four months dead, it did not seem to fit. Where had she lain? Yuichi looked down to two small patches of threadbare carpet in front of the chair. It didn't matter, the police would work it out.

It was finished, ready to close yet age and the room's dankness conspired against her knees. Three pm, three hours to wander until Takeshi returns. Perhaps I will wait, sit for a while.

The chair was hard but comfortable, a western design with scallops for her buttocks. With the window open the late afternoon breeze eventually turned cold on her shoulders. She couldn't close it, had to let the room air, so she lifted the chair to move it back against the wall. Arthritic fingers failed, the chair slipping from her grip to fall across the table. Something dislodged itself, rolled to a stop at her feet. A small, dark disc. Yuichi picked it up. Where did it come from? She couldn't see any part of the table missing or broken. Takeshi was strict and the police were firmer, no theft or breakages permitted. She heard him coming down the corridor. She slid the disc into her pocket with her tack rag just as his face popped round the doorway.

"I hope you did not work too hard today. A simple one after that run of bad, you could do with a little rest."

"It was exceptionally clean Takeshi-san."

"They said she hardly ate or came out of her room, she wasn't really here anyway. I will drive you home, I have the van outside."

My apartment's no larger than hers, a single room with bathroom and kitchenette. I left the curtains open this morning, the ten story J-pop neon now lighting the apartment as day. I used to track the days by name, then by the work that came, now by the pain. My back says it's mid-week, by the time my legs scream it will be my rest day.

I pour a lukewarm cup of tea and sit heavily opposite the low cabinet. His face stares back from the frame younger, confident, proudly in love. I can't remember why I keep it, his confidence and strength a shattered lie bringing the rest of my world down when he left.

I carefully fold my clothes and place them on the floor ready for tomorrow. The disc falls, rolls a short distance to stop in the cracked linoleum. I pick it up and absent mindedly spin it. Thin, smooth and cool to the touch, a curiosity from a dead woman to a dying one.

The disc is strangely captivating sliding across my palm; I really should return it to the police, let it lie unclaimed for a year then be incinerated. Would it hurt just this once to hold onto something, a small reminder of a life passed unnoticed? I place the disc between the picture frames.

Small reminders, all that was left for many, all that is left me. His was the one love, enough while it lasted. I should forgive, should understand the pain to him was as great as mine, but time has entombed his fragility in the walls of my sorrow.

A six year old's pretend scowl stares out at me. Ashima at cherry blossom time in the avenue, rose colored petals at her feet. The disc changes unnoticed from deep indigo to dark blue. Oh how Ashima demanded that costume, the pins and clips bunching the sack-like kimono away from the camera's telltale eye until her delight with the final picture. Another perfect day in a perfect life, the perfect little family safe inside the salary man bubble dissolving a week later as Ashima lay broken at the bottom of the stairs and he abandoned me to my fate.

The dark blue pales with my tears, small hesitant travelers down the lined and pockmarked landscape of experience. Each night I cry, each night I mourn for her, for forty empty years and the lives stolen from me. Pale blue rises unnoticed to white as I screw my eyes closed struggling to bring a scrap of Ashima's laughter back, her smell, the strength in a child's hug. I fail as I always do, screaming silent curses to my impotent ancestors.

"Mummy, why are you crying?"

Why do they taunt me, using even her memory to dangle the ravings of a shattered mind before me?

"Open your eyes, the blossoms are falling and the sky is blue."

Perfumed scent enfolds me, the breeze gently tousling my hair. My eyes open to a clear day, cherry blossom avenue, the impossible.

"Ashima? What are you doing here?"

"It's my birthday, you promised I could cosplay."

"No, no I mean you're here? You are aren't you?"

"Silly, the costume's not that good."

The white soars to rainbow incandescence, the beauty lost to unseeing eyes.

"How long do we have?"

"Today and tomorrow and the next and forever and ever."

Ashima bounds over, wrapping her arms around me. Strong arms, apple scented hair, soft cheeks.

"I want the photo first and then the pandas, the little baby ones."

Grabbing my hand she pulls me to my feet.

"Can I have some ice-cream? Just a little, I promise I won't spoil dinner."

"Of course, of course you can."

"Good. You can have the vanilla, I'll eat the strawberry. I love you mummy."

"I love you too sweetheart."

The disc glows translucent, Yuichi as stone in the chair unmoving, unseeing, unaware. Night falls into day back to neon night to weeks, an unnoticed procession as it glows, as Yuichi remains.

Yuichi drew her last breath and was stilled.

The disc fades to deep indigo and waits.

END

ECHOES

THE MAN AT immigration inspects my documents along with my bags and my very person in minute detail. Although disconcerting it is expected. I am their first.

"It all seems in order. Welcome to Earth."

"Thank you."

"I saw the newscasts. Terrible tragedy."

"It's regrettable dying far from home and kin."

"That's what I meant."

My driver whisks me from the spaceport. It gives them a chance to keep an eye on me without being too obvious. Not that I'm a threat. They're all curious, cursed with overactive imaginations, a boundless entertainment industry and insatiable emotional appetites. I don't want to be here, thankfully I only have to put up with it for a day or two. I just have to remember not to touch anyone.

Sweaty and gap toothed the driver stares at me through the partition.

"I haven't seen your type before."

"We don't travel much."

"Too nice at home eh? Well we've got some stuff too, big things like Pyramids and even some lions. You should go see."

"Maybe next time."

"I saw it you know. Nasty, going all that way then that."

Everyone probably saw the recordings. It was no use, they'd all want to tell me so I might as well get used to it.

"Yes."

"How many died, I mean of your lot?"

"Three hundred."

"That any of ours survived was a miracle, pure miracle."

"You're a tough species."

"Couldn't understand it."

"What?"

"How only two made it. To go through it all, survive the crash then die later, that's rough."

How could I tell her, make any of them understand? We wanted to help but there had to be precautions. I'd been first there dragging all of them out bare handed then those three broken ones more dead than alive. I was paying the price for my recklessness.

"We mourned yours as we mourned our own."

"Tragic loss for the families, their friends."

"Yes, our world's very tight knit, very close."

"That too."

They'd been told I was coming to make sure they were prepared. It was to be just me and the person behind each door yet the streets were still closed off. We pulled up in front of a small blue-gray box, flaking paint and tall thin plants obscuring the ground.

"How long will you be?"

"Depends. Five seconds, five hours. Just wait."

The porch steps creaked under me, the doorbell needed to be pressed twice to work. He was older than I recalled, hair thinner and grayed, stoop shouldered. Behind him the grandfather clock stood, that one ostentatious anachronism he couldn't shake.

"Adam Wright?"

"Yes."

"I am —"

"I know."

He opened the screen door, offered me his hand. I removed my glove, grasped his firmly just as the clock started to strike five.

— Dad!

— Indrani? Indrani my poor, poor baby girl.

— Don't go all soft on me now.

— You're back, back home.

— No, you know why I'm here, you know what they told you.

— Why did you have to go? You should have stayed here where it's safe.

— It's all I ever wanted. I was no idiot, I knew what it might cost. I was happy dad, totally in love with what I did. I wouldn't change a thing even now, and you made it happen.

— Me?

— All those years after mum died you were alone, you took care of me, encouraged me, made me think I could own the stars. You put me where I could follow my dreams, all the while putting yourself last. I've never said thank you properly. It's why I'm here, to say thank you, thank you for everything.

— You don't have to, I'm your father. What else could I have done?

— You could have done anything at all. All my life I wanted to thank you but somehow I never managed, never found the time or the words. Now I have to.

— Have to?

— It was the only regret I had, the only thing I'd left undone. It was all I was thinking of when he pulled me clear, when I died. It's torturing him having me here, having it unsaid. They're not built for it we're … we're too intense.

— What happens now when you, I mean he leaves? Do you die again?

—I can't, you die once then that's it. But this echo has to leave him or he'll be in pain his whole life. I'm luckier than most, I've had the chance to put things right. He can be released, I can fade away.

— And me?

— You can't change the past.

— Will it hurt?

— No. Just let go and that's it. On. Off. Simple.

— I love you Indrani.

— I know dad, I always knew. And I love you.

He released my hand as the clock finished striking five, his face quivering as the emotion worked its way through him. My headache and chest pains reduced. She's gone, faded and left. He extended his hand again then pulled it away.

"I'm sorry, I forgot. I'm glad you made the effort."

"I had no choice, your daughter was insistent."

"She's gone?"

"Yes."

"And you're better?"

"Somewhat, I have more to see."

"I figured you might. I'm sorry for your pain, those people of yours who died."

When I left the next one it was too late to see the last, too early for my rituals. I was feeling better but the last weighed heavily upon me. I was hungry, thirsty and tired.

The driver pulled up next to a garish yellow and red neon sign.

"This will do, I can get them to give us the food in the car instead if you want."

Only one or two people were inside. I glanced to the left, the security tail seemed to be keen to rest.

"They have food that is not from an animal?"

She pulled out a piece of paper.

"These ones, anything with the word 'vegan'. You squeamish?"

"No, let's just say I get a ... bad vibe from it."

I went in, squeezed into a booth in the far corner and ordered. My food arrived. Nutritious perhaps, appealing not.

I was trying to wipe off a white liquid that had oozed onto my gloves when I became aware of an adult male sitting opposite me staring nervously, intimidated by something near me. I looked around. There was nothing, just myself.

"You're one of them?"

"One of what?"

"An amortal."

They'd called us that when we met. A simplistic misleading meme that had been no end of trouble.

"Yes but I'm not amortal. It's the wrong word."

"It doesn't matter, a rose by any other name. You all look alike don't you?"

"No, it's just your differences are so dramatic."

"It's true isn't it, the rumors?"

"What is?"

"You talk to the dead."

"It is and it isn't, depends what you mean."

"No one really dies do they, you take on their memory, their spirit when they go."

"Among our own people yes, you could say that. But you do too, your memories, it's just … different."

"But that's why you're here. Bringing those three back to their families, making them live again."

"No, that's not quite —"

He shoved a picture at me, his purple splotched hand shaking. A woman and two young children smiled out at me through creases and stains.

"My family, they were all I had. You got a family?"

"Offspring? Yes, and parents."

"Then you understand. I killed them twenty years ago."

"You killed them?"

"I was driving home. I'd been drinking and picked them up. There was an accident. I lived, they died."

"I'm sorry."

"I lost it all when I lost them. Not an hour passes I don't think of them."

"It sounds like a horrible life, is there —"

"Bring them back."

"What?"

"Bring them back now like you did the others."

"I can't."

"Don't lie! I know you can, so do it."

"You don't understand, no one comes back it's just echoes. Even if I wanted to I couldn't, I wasn't there when they died."

His face turned red, one arm rising holding a knife.

"It's not fair bringing back the others and not mine. You're like the rest of them, disrespecting and discriminating me! So help me if you don't bring them back right now I'll …"

The knife clattered to the floor as he slumped to the table. The uniforms took him away, my driver staring at me.

"I'm sorry, my fault. Didn't pick him soon enough."

"No real harm done."

"A lot of people think that way."

"And you?"

She opened the car door.

"Hardly. Live once, die once, all over. Who'd want to come back to this shit hole?"

They'd increased the guard overnight, I stepped from my room to an escort of a dozen men. So much for discretion.

"They heard what happened, don't want a repeat."

"Guess you'll be glad to get rid of me."

"No, I've had worse. The Pope, now that's another thing. He thinks you're the antichrist."

"What's a pope?"

"Erin Carlson?"

"Yes, I've been expecting you. Come in."

She ushered me into a neat, sparsely furnished space. She sat out of arm's reach.

"Thank you for seeing me."

"It's no trouble. I have a few questions."

"If it will help."

"It will. Why?"

"Why what?"

"Why you."

"Pure chance. When the ship malfunctioned the escape pod crashed into my house. No other reason."

"No, that's not what I meant. Why'd they give their echoes to you?"

"They didn't actually give them. It was an accident."

"How?"

"I didn't think, I just reacted. I didn't know who crashed so I didn't take any precautions, just went straight in and pulled the five of them out before it burnt up. Everyone else just stood around and by the time I realized it was too late."

"And you had all five of them in you?"

"Initially. The two who survived I was able to give theirs back, but the other three were impossible."

"Why?"

"If the echo comes across with unfinished business it stays with the host and drives them until it's finished, then it fades and releases. All three of them died with unfinished business."

"But it's never really gone is it?"

"Where'd you hear that?"

"Brendan. He spent years with your people studying, thinking, watching."

"It's true. Once the echo's satisfied it leaves but the ... it's hard to find the words ... the essence or flavor still remains. Nothing specific just impressions, generalities, but then again more."

"Dead but truly never forgotten?"

"Yes, perhaps that will do."

"Brendan must be giving you trouble."

"Yes, his emotional state is far above even your norms."

"Your people, they quarantined you for this?"

"They had no choice. We can't risk contamination."

"You want to grip my hand, be done with him?"

I started to remove my gloves.

"Of course."

"I don't. I want the other way, the way of your people."

"No, that's not permissible."

"It's either that or Brendan stays with you until you die."

There was no choice. I couldn't continue like this.

"Very well. But don't watch me change, the process is confronting. I'll ... Brendan will let you know when I've changed."

She closed her eyes and I let go. It hurt enough morphing to one of my own, but changing into this creature was an absurd and painful struggle. Our masses weren't even close, I had to lose a few inches height to compensate. She'd never know.

Of course the stupid bitch wouldn't, I only married her so I'd have a decent body on tap if I couldn't get lucky. What she had in looks she lost in brains.

"Erin. I'm here."

"Brendan. You look good dead, it suits you."

"What do you want?"

"Me? You're the echo."

"Oh yeah, that. Just died thinking what a useless bitch you were, how you'd ruined my life and how much I'd miss telling you that."

"That all?"

"Isn't it enough? You've hardly got room in your head for your name never mind anything else. I'm surprised you remembered anything I said."

"Depends if I wanted to."

"You're like a faulty computer, can't remember anything unless I punch it in a few times."

"You enjoyed that didn't you?"

"Are you kidding? Come home, bang you senseless, punch the shit out of you then go and do your little sister. It was the best."

"You'll pay for that."

"How, you forgotten I'm dead? Shame, I was going to get rid of you when I got back, it's not even funny anymore."

Erin reached behind her, lifted the Taser and fired. Brendan collapsed to the floor, Erin sending two more shots into him for good measure. Methodically she removed the darts, bound his wrists and ankles, taped over his mouth and waited until he came around.

"Brendan?"

He nodded, face up.

She fired the Taser point blank into his groin.

Accompanied by muffled screaming she went to the kitchen, returning with a cup of coffee and the knife block.

"Brendan?"

He nodded, this time from the fetal position.

She sat, placed her feet on his face.

"That was just for fun, help me calm down. I can't tell you how excited I was when I heard you were coming back. I mean, I was so glad you died but it was too clean and neat if you know what I mean."

She moved her feet slightly, driving a stiletto into his nostril. Funny how such a small thing could control him but then again he'd always been controlled by small things.

"You never noticed me change. While you were away I got help, got my respect and strength back. I was heartbroken when I heard you died, the thought of dragging you through court was delicious but even that you tried to take from me."

A small twist brought his face towards her. She resisted the temptation to take out an eye with the other heel, contenting herself with scouring his forehead, seeing exactly at which point blood flowed or bone showed.

"Charles is such a thorough solicitor. Do you know your host isn't legally a person on earth? Or that we don't have an extradition treaty with them? No? Pity."

She leant in, let the tiniest drop of spittle fall.

"As far as this world's concerned you're dead, and I can't get charged for killing a dead person now can I? But we both know as long as he lives you live whether you're wearing his body or not."

Brendan twisted slightly, nearly tearing his nose open. Erin pulled on a pair of elbow length rubber gloves.

"No, I'm afraid that's no use. You'll find the Taser's charge will stop you shifting back for a couple of days. That should be more than long enough."

She took the rod from the block and slowly started to sharpen the paring knife.

"You're right of course, I never was much of a cook. My knife work was never up to scratch. But we've got all day, so much to catch up on, so many memories to relive."

END

HOT DOG

"WHAT LINE OF business are you in Mr. Patheson?"

Ugly fucking hairy ape-woman, what do you know of business? Just rent me the space and be done with it. You'll find out my business soon enough.

"Entertainment Cindii, a little import export on the side."

"I see."

No you don't, none of your ugly symmetrical air-breathing bastard kind ever has.

"So will this place do? City center, three hundred fifty square meters, fifth level basement with loading ramp and goods elevator."

Idiot. If it lasts a week it's enough.

"How much again?"

"Two and a quarter on a three plus three lease."

"It's perfect."

Hot. Dog. Hotdog. What garbage is this? I've had constipation, flatulence and arrhythmia eating this factory produced swill they call food. No wonder they all smell like shit, fat assed sweaty bodied perverts. White bun, red thing smothered in yellow vomit and crisp brown shards. It bears a passing resemblance to a dog's dick on a hot day and I wouldn't put it past one of these morons to have tried eating that. Sex obsessed losers, everything comes back to penis envy or pussy strike. The universe'll be better off without them.

"Turn around slow and quiet. Do as I say and you won't get hurt."

I turn. It's only a knife, like I'm fucking scared? I haven't got time for this but I'm bored. This stupid ape's mind's as easy to control as the rest of them.

"Strip."

He does as he's told, I leave his eyes and mind unlocked to watch the show. It's always more fun that way.

"Cut off your dick."

The horror on his face is wonderful, I toy with opening his vocal chords but the mall's too close. It's a lot of blood for such a small pink thing. What the fuck. I hand him the hotdog.

"Stick it in this."

I feel like laughing for the first time today, he knows what's coming and can't stop it. The more his eyes plead the better it gets. Just hope he doesn't bleed out too soon.

"Enjoy your lunch, make sure to eat it all."

I stay for the first few bites enjoying feeling his mind skittering to insanity. I turn the corner into the mall and release him, the scream rising above the traffic. Shame I haven't more time, twelve billion of them and they're all mine.

The basement's perfect. Anywhere would have done but I'm a showman, an artist, and my viewing audience demands a spectacle. At least for the first few hours. Nodes across the world solve that, my direct feed's a subscriber perk.

I take the lines and lay them on the floor in two one hundred and fifty square meter rectangles. I connect the brackets and they're live, just awaiting the command. Indestructible, they'll stay through it all.

It's a good hill, nice view of the city and safe for the first hour or so. I slide open the van's freezer and she hands me a Magnum. She doesn't need the rest of her body and it's a tight fit anyway, so waistline up's all that's there. Simple stupid ape biology, so easy to keep alive. I let her cry to see how long the icicles get but that voice is grating. The ice-cream's nice, one thing from this planet of shit.

"How's that monthly sales target now Cindii? Tell you what, I'll let you watch the show."

I put her on the grass facing away from my chair. She's just the right height. I sit down, place a boot on each shoulder and settle in.

I'd toyed with sequencing. What first, the portal 10,000 meters undersea in the Dokarzha Deeps or the one in Betelgeuse's core? It's a simulcast, so it's both at once. I throw the mental switch.

It's beautiful, city erased as two giant columns of water and plasma erupt and mix to hyper-steam, the shock wave turning everything to dust for five kilometers as the columns soar, tearing the Earth up and flinging it to the four winds. Every nanosecond recorded and live streamed, every terror stricken pained instant before oblivion lifted from the minds of seven million naked apes, as it would be for them all as the whole planet was scoured, steamed, cleansed.

The earth beneath me trembles as the old fault lines awake, the thrusting magma flows seeking the surface.

What the fuck, I've got time. I flip on my shield and decide to stay. I let her scream, every movie needs a soundtrack.

And I need a holiday.

END

CALL ME

THE TECHNICIAN SQUINTS his pale blue eyes, twists a screwdriver to slot home a coupling.

Frank Garrity was running late as he stepped outside and checked his mobile. The taxi ranks were empty but there were a few Uber rides around. It was a rushed trip and in all the hurry at the building site he'd just managed to change into his suit. He looked down, brown steel caps laughing where black Florsheims should be.

Sonia stared out the window as the car crawled through the city. Was that a suit wearing steel capped boots? The driver craned her neck back.

"You ok if I don't pick up share rides? Heard some bad stories lately."

"Fine by me, I'm in a hurry."

Self check-in was down so Frank joined the economy queue. They opened the business class counter to economy passengers, a forlorn effort given the snaking line behind him. He'd made it to the front when there was a gasp and clatter. Turning he saw an old lady trying unsuccessfully to pick up her walking stick. No one lifted a hand to help, the man between them staring at his watch. Frank stepped around him.

"They should have a special lane."

"I'm fine. Looks like someone's cut in front of you."

Frank turned as the watch checker scurried to the counter.

"What's a few minutes?"

Thankfully business class got preferential treatment, small compensation for the two hour packed flight to Townsville. The counter attendant handed Sonia her boarding pass.

"You're boarding through gate twenty three in approximately ninety minutes, seat 1B. Have a pleasant flight."

"QF 978?"

The man at the counter stared at the monitor, his blue eyes barely concealing his irritation.

"Is there a problem?"

"Just the usual, it's over booked."

A boarding slip shot onto the counter.

"Economy's full so I've put you in business."

"Is it going to cost me?"

"No, nothing. Seat 4B, boarding in an hour and a half from gate twenty three. Pleasant flight Mr. Garrity."

The security checkpoint was an overcrowded nightmare. Tempers frayed as people were sent back through for coins in pockets, mobile phones, even belts. A man was pulled aside, told to take off his boots. Sonia went through, extracted her carry-on and headed for the escalator.

Frank made his way back around through the scanner. Boots back on he grabbed his grip before jumping on the escalator. They were three deep on each step families, businessmen and holiday makers jam packed together. An old couple at the top stumbled off, her scarf trailing on the floor as they walked away.

Frank made the top of the escalator and turned left through the food court to the newsagent.

"Your coffee."

She cleared a small space on the table and placed the mug down in front of Sonia. Sonia had toyed with going into the club but lately it was filled with noisy families. A man sailed towards her engrossed in his newspaper, arm high passing over her head, jacket brushing the edge of her table. A woman pulled a chair up next to the old man opposite. It's definitely better out here, the people watching's more fun.

Frank's eyes were fixed to the sports page as he hurried to the departure lounge. Bunch of losers, beaten by Bangladesh four nil. In the old days we would've routed them but now we can't even lose by less than an innings.

He finished the paper in disgust, page after page of bad news. The country's just an open pit mine populated by Netflix junkies.

"QF 978 is now ready for boarding, would business class passengers proceed to gate twenty three."

Frank folded the paper then stood. He thought about keeping it then, deciding against it, dropped it on the chair behind him before joining the queue.

The boarding call caught Sonia unawares. She was last in business class, just settling into her seat as economy was called. Probably going to be a bad flight, the old lady next to me in 1A looks worried, apprehensive.

"You too?"

The old man in 4A nodded.

"My wife's in 1A, they wouldn't put us together it was this or get bumped."

"That's rough."

"No kidding. She doesn't like flying, too much tv, those air crash shows."

"You should be together."

"That's what I said."

The blue eyed business class steward leant across.

"You'd prefer to sit together sir?"

"Of course, but they said it couldn't be done."

"Well that was down there and this is my flight. If you're willing to shift to 1A Mr. Garrity we can fix it easy enough."

"Sure, one seat's as good as another."

Sonia tried not to notice him. Male, mid-thirties, business suit and not too hard on the eyes. I'm not in the market, it's barely two years since Peter died and no matter what Julie says it's too early. 'You're taking too long,' she'd scolded a week ago 'no-one's talking about a relationship here just go find a piece of beefcake and disappear for a few days.' She shook her head, tried to appear nonchalant.

He held out his hand.

"I'm Frank. Sorry if I startled you."

"Sonia. You didn't, I was just lost in thought. Off to Townsville?" She kicked herself as she said it.

"Not much choice now, this makes only one stop." He smiled. "Business or pleasure?"

"Business. You?"

"Same, two days. I'm there so often it feels like home."

"Sounds awful."

"It's not too bad, I've got a regular room at Jupiter's and most of them know me."

"Jupiter's? I'm booked there too, isn't that a —"

The pain exploding in Sonia's head blocked everything out, pitching her forwards driving her head between her knees. She caught a glimpse of Frank arched backwards, mouth open before the world dissolved in a blue-gold haze then faded to black.

"You too?"

The old man in 4A nodded.

"My wife's in 1A, they wouldn't put us together it was this or get bumped."

"That's rough."

"No kidding. She doesn't like flying, too much tv, those air crash shows."

"You should be together."

"That's what I said."

The business class stewardess leant across. A petite blonde, she'd been flashing her beacon-like emerald green eyes at Frank since he boarded.

"You'd prefer to sit together sir?"

"Of course, but they said it couldn't be done."

"Well that was down there and this is my flight. If you're willing to shift to 4D Mr. Garrity we can fix it easy enough."

"Sure, one seat's as good as another."

The aircraft started to push back, the terminal lights receding as Frank stared out the window. A howling whine burst through his ears, a searing pain through his head sending him arching back into his seat as the blue-gold light changed to black then oblivion.

The old man's got gorgeous blue eyes.

"Sorry?"

"They've just called QF 978. You'd better hurry."

Sonia gulped down her remaining coffee, stood hurriedly.

"Thanks."

She didn't notice him until she blundered into him, sending him to the floor.

"Oh god I'm sorry."

He picked himself up, reached down to get her carry-on and boarding pass. He's quite tall, attractive and well-built if a little disheveled. The hint of a six pack winked from above his belt; she felt his eyes follow hers.

"It's quite alright," he said tucking his shirt back in "these queues are always a fight anyway ..." looking at her boarding pass "Mrs. Nicolas."

"I should pay more attention. And it's Sonia."

"Pleased to meet you Sonia, I'm Frank."

"Going all the way?" Damn you Julie.

"As far as I can but I think it stops in Townsville."

"Business?"

"Yeah, couple of days. You?"

"Same. I'm there so often Jupiter's should put my name on the door."

"Jupiter's? I'm there all the time but I've never —"

The pain was overwhelming, driving Sonia to her knees screaming as the world turned blue-gold then faded away.

Frank's eyes were fixed to the sports page as he hurried to the departure lounge. Bunch of losers, beaten by Bangladesh four nil. In the old days we would've routed them but now we can't even lose by less than an innings.

He finished the paper in disgust, page after page of bad news. The country's just an open pit mine populated by Netflix junkies.

"QF 978 is now ready for boarding, would business class passengers proceed to gate twenty three."

Frank folded the paper then stood.

"Excuse me."

Frank looked to the short, green eyed woman seated behind him. "Yes?"

"Is that today's Courier Mail?"

"Yes."

"Do you mind if I have it? Things are a bit tight."

Frank handed the paper to her.

"They give them away on board."

"I'm not flying, I'm waiting for someone."

Business class boarding was over so Frank joined the economy queue. Funny woman, the parking alone would get her a month's subscription. It was an assault on his senses, the noise, the lights, a debilitating but familiar cacophony pounding him to unconsciousness.

"Your coffee."

He placed the cup and saucer down near the edge of the table in front of Sonia, smiled with ice blue eyes then walked away. Sonia had toyed with going into the club but lately it was filled with noisy families. A man sailed towards her engrossed in his newspaper, arm passing over her head, jacket catching the saucer sending the cup smashing to the floor. He spun to face her.

"I'm sorry I …"

He looked hauntingly familiar, triggering a misty soup of fear, love, belonging and hatred in her head.

"Sonia?"

It came back in stereo, one channel of ambition, success and sharing, the other in pale solitary reflection.

"Frank? It's still happening?"

"Yes," glancing at his paper "it's 2027? We've gone that far back?"

She grabbed his hand, squeezed hard.

"Keep fighting, it's all we can do."

"I know it's just —"

The light and pain blew them to blackness.

"Your coffee."

The waitress stood looking at her, a cup of coffee in one hand, dishrag in the other. Why do her green eyes give me the jitters? The waitress regarded the table littered with food scraps and spilt coffee distastefully.

"This is awful, it should have been cleaned earlier." The table behind her emptied; the waitress gave it a cursory wipe, putting Sonia's coffee down in the middle.

"Will this do? It's cleaner and out of the way."

Sonia moved across.

"Yes thank you it's fine."

Sonia had toyed with going into the club but lately it was … she stopped in mid-thought, waves of déjà vu washing over her. What was it, a thought, a name, a face? A man hurried past engrossed in his newspaper, stopped and stared briefly at the seat she'd vacated then with a shake of his head walked away.

Sonia stood, raised one arm as if to go off in pursuit then spasmed as the as the world exploded blue-gold.

Frank made his way back around through the scanner. Boots back on he grabbed his grip before jumping on the escalator. They were three deep on each step families, businessmen and holiday makers jam packed together. An old man and woman fell to the floor at the top, her scarf jammed in the mechanism. Someone bent down to help, everyone else ignoring them and hurrying off. Frank made it to the top just in time to help pick them up.

"She's fine, thank you." the old man said glancing quickly through blue eyes before hurrying away.

Frank turned, reeled, then dragged Sonia away.

"Frank?"

"How far back are we?"

"I don't know, it's all hazy I can't remember."

"They're still trying."

"To keep us apart?"

"Or together, I've no idea but they're still trying."

"It's getting shorter."

"We're down to minutes, maybe less."

"What do we do?"

"Have to break the pattern, do something different."

"Like what?"

They fell as one in a crumpled heap.

"QF 978?"

The girl at the counter stared at the monitor, her green eyes barely concealing her irritation.

"Is there a problem?"

"Just the usual, it's over booked."

A boarding slip shot onto the counter.

"I've had to change your seat, it's not your preferred one but it will do. Seat 42J, boarding in an hour and a half from gate twenty three. Pleasant flight Mr. Garrity."

Frank walked towards security pensive and worried. I feel like a fight, no, like I'm in a fight, no, no more like I should be … the grayness evaporated and he remembered, crystal clear he remembered why just before the world collapsed.

Self check-in was down so Frank joined the economy queue. They opened the business class counter to economy passengers, a forlorn effort given the snaking line behind him. He'd made it to the front when there was a gasp and clatter. Turning he saw an old lady trying unsuccessfully to pick up her walking stick. A young boy stooped, picked it up and took the old lady by the arm.

"Thank you."

"It's no trouble."

He looked straight at Frank with a set of ice blue eyes.

"Go to business class check in sir, help speed it along."

"Thanks." Frank said, moving away.

Thankfully business class got preferential treatment, small compensation for the packed two hour flight to Townsville. The counter attendant handed Sonia her boarding pass.

"You're boarding through gate twenty three in approximately ninety minutes, seat 1B. Have a pleasant flight."

Sonia turned, bumped face first into Frank. This time recognition was instant. She grabbed him, dragged him away.

"It's still going, it's getting earlier."

Frank's face was ashen.

"Listen. I know why it's here, it's this flight."

"What is?"

"Us, the first time. It's when we met."

"Then they've won."

"No they haven't. They know nothing about before. If we don't meet on this flight they'll think it's finished, but we can fool them."

"How?"

"My number, do you remember my number?"

"Yes, yes I think so."

"Good. Call me, just call. You never did before tomorrow, just make one call and we can reset it."

"When?"

"Before the flight, as early as you can. We've got to miss the flight. If either of us gets on it alone it's over. Can you do it?"

"Yes, I think —"

This time the world faded to malevolent black.

The technician squints her emerald green eyes, twists a screwdriver to release a coupling.

Frank Garrity was running late as he stepped outside and checked his mobile. The taxi ranks were empty and his mobile was playing up. He fidgeted, danced from foot to foot. Looks like I'm going to miss the flight.

Sonia stared out the window as the car crawled through the city. Was that a suit wearing steel capped boots? The driver craned her neck back.

"You ok if I don't pick up share rides? Heard some bad stories lately."

"Fine by me, I'm in a hurry."

Something tugged at her; she picked up her mobile and dialed. Nothing happened.

"Damn, no coverage."

"Been like that all day."

She turned her mobile off, put it in her carry on.

"Guess I could use some peace and quiet."

"Couldn't we all."

The driver looked back, emerald green eyes reflected in the mirror.

"Don't worry, I'll get you there on time. Can't have you missing that flight can we?"

END

RECALL

"A THOUSAND BUCKS."

Dave knew his mark. Ratface didn't flinch.

"Cash?"

"Always."

"Done deal. How long?"

"Two hours."

Dave turned to me as ratface walked away.

"Go get started, I'll back the truck up."

I did a quick inventory, the bed sit wasn't big but it was worth more. So much for respecting the elderly. A photo of ratface and a woman stared out from a cluttered table. The photo found its way to my tin, the frame to salvage.

Two hours later we left ratface and the real estate agent shrinking in the mirrors. Dave glanced at the tin on my lap.

"Usual?"

"Yeah. Photos, letters, junk."

"Beats me why you want it."

"Every man needs a hobby."

He ran the red light whistling happily. The Royal Doulton would make him a good return.

"Whatever."

I turned out the tin at home. The letters, photos and ticket stubs would go to my sister at the local history association. I kept the old nib pen, a relic I knew I could shift for a few dollars. And the watch.

An old Timex digital, worn but clean with a dogeared leather band. I wiped off the dust. It bore an inscription 'June. '59' just above the battery cover. I slipped it into my pocket.

"Fifteen dollars."

"You serious Erin?"

She took the loupe from her eye, gave me a doleful stare.

"What else. It's maybe worth thirty retail, parts or working, and it won't shift for ages. I've gotta keep my margins. And the crap inscription don't help."

"What?"

"Lookit. 'June '59'. Timex didn't do digitals till the seventies. Either someone got the year wrong by a few decades or your lady was fifty nine when she got it. Believe me, none of my customers wanna know how old their ladies are."

"Fifteen dollars?"

"And it's charity even if it works."

She took off the battery cover, a small rusted disc falling out. "CR92, CR92" she muttered rummaging through a drawer until she emerged with the disc's shiny twin. She replaced battery and cover to be rewarded by a gentle chime.

She held it closer to tap a blue button on one side.

"So it works, but this isn't standard and does nothing. Maybe now it's worth ten."

I snatched it back.

"No thanks, I'll keep it. How much for the battery?"

"Like I said, I'm feeling charitable. Just come back with something valuable next time."

I toweled off after my shower, slipped on my boxers and settled down for the game. I was early so I put the panel on mute and picked up the watch. I put it on, threaded the strap through the buckle. It felt solid, like it belonged. I still couldn't figure out how to set the time so I just kept playing with it. I pushed the blue button down and held it.

The room imploded to a black and white checked cube then to a glass tube, a surprised woman in a lab coat looking at me. She jabbed a panel beside her. Something burned my nose and throat, the room melting to black. I awoke to cream-lilac tiled surfaces, a desk, an empty chair on one side and me in another opposite. The chill through my boxers was intense. The watch was gone.

A gap in the wall closed behind a short man. He sat opposite me, placed a small box to to one side and the watch to the other.

"Where did you get this?"

"I want my lawyer."

"There are none."

"I know my rights. Lawyer. Phone call."

"You have none. Not here. Not now."

"You military?"

"Worse."

He pointed to the watch.

"Where did you get this?"

I'd been in this position before, law in front and me on the wrong side of it. He was too calm, too dispassionate. He wanted to know about the watch? Fine. I told him.

"Her address?"

"Twenty eight Highview."

"Time, date you were there?"

"Ten August, about two pm."

"Which year?"

"This year."

"Humor me. Which year?"

"Two thousand eleven."

He stood.

"Wait."

Like I could go anywhere. My feet were glued to the floor.

He came back.

"It checks out."

"Of course it does. Now what?"

He stayed silent.

"When is this?"

"How'd you guess?"

"No one has walls that open and close and I've never heard of anyone's feet being stuck down without cuffs or chains. How far?"

"Centuries."

"Whose watch was it?"

"One of ours."

"He's stuck back there?"

"No. Sometimes we don't place them properly. She's dead. Just waited too long to hit recall."

"Must've liked it."

"Perhaps. It happens."

"Will I like it here?"

"No."

"No?"

"Too different. You'd be useless."

"Always room if a guy can push a broom, pull a beer."

"Not here, not now."

"So?"

"A choice. You can stay, but for your own sanity we'd have to ... reset ... your memories."

"You mean erase."

"Yes."

"Or?"

"Send you back."

"No memory reset?"

"No need. Who'll believe you?"

He slid the small box across.

"Take one. When you get back you're drunk. In a month it will just be a bad dream."

"Option two then."

The tube shifted rapidly to cube then pitch black. I took one step and fell face first into the soaking earth, rising to my knees covered in putrid mud. To each side faint clicks and rattles, metal on metal, dull thud of boots on wood through the darkness.

The sky turned phosphorescent as the first shells exploded over Ypres.

END

WOOD FOR THE TREES

DANIELA LEANT OVER the rail, gazing at the room full of machinery. She squeezed the nape of her neck, grinned wryly then turned.

"That's it Ted, shut it down."

"Damn, I thought we finally had it."

"It's just science, some theories are right, some are wrong. Shame this one's taken thirty nine years."

"You lasted longer than the rest."

"You mean they're quicker than me? Maybe I'm just too stubborn."

"What now?"

She shrugged.

"Mark it all for scrap, clear it out before the charges pile up. Everything else can wait."

The night traffic was light, freeway in front empty, Melbourne's lights fading slowly behind. Always the same, as it ever was and, she now knew, as it always would be. The headlights swayed gently in time with Benny Goodman. She turned the radio up. I need a holiday to clear my head, perhaps Europe or the States. A week or two in the air, evening deck promenades over the Pacific, the whisper of silk through air, the clink of champagne flutes at four thousand feet. The clipboard slid across the bench seat, tapping her thigh. Four billion people don't know hard I've tried, nothing's changed for them. She lifted the clipboard, sent the litany of failure spinning out the window into darkness.

Daniela pulled into her driveway, turned off the car letting the night envelop her. What was the old saying, the end of a thing is better than its beginning? Whatever. She got out, leant against the '19 Bel Air's fins and gazed up. The twin moons shone down, scudding silver-blue discs shepherding iridescent rings across the heavens. Perfect as always. Daniela sighed, finally smiled. Why did I ever want to change it anyway?.

END

ABOUT THE AUTHOR

Ishmael A Soledad has read and watched science fiction since before he went to school and thought it was time to give back instead of just taking. Continuing to write short fiction he is currently working on his first novel. He lives in Brisbane, Australia with his long-suffering wife and psychotic cat.

You can connect with him at

Website : ishmaeltheauthor.com

Twitter : @Ishmael_Soledad

Goodreads :   https://www.goodreads.com/